SURVIVAL
HOUSE

SURVIVAL HOUSE

Stories by

WENDELL MAYO

STEPHEN F. AUSTIN STATE UNIVERSITY PRESS

For information about special discounts for bulk purchases, contact Distribution at sfapress@sfasu.edu or 1-936-468-1078

Book Design by: Emily Townsend
Cover Design by: Emily Townsend
Cover Image: "Exterior, Apple II House," with permission of Danny Bradbury
Back Cover Image: "Miss Atomic Bomb, 1957," with permission of the Las Vegas Convention and Visitors Authority

ISBN: 978-1-62288-189-5

First Edition

Advance Praise for *Survival House*

Mayo's storytelling voice–explosively imaginative, rich with dark laughter, addictively readable–speaks for our historical moment. *Survival House* overlays the Cold War with its resurgent threat today. The anxieties and signature events of the nuclear age, then and now, are reframed as personal, domestic, and small-town dramas gone wildly weird, as if a lid of familiarity were blown off a kettle of surreal truths. In Mayo's moribund yet tenderly depicted Rust Belt, a town festival celebrates the nuclear end of humanity; and a hilarious but ominous Russian-themed bar opens in Whitehouse, Ohio. From the ruins of a Soviet nuclear facility emerges an epiphany about the global violence's source in the human heart. With satirical and lyric virtuosity, Mayo conjures an essential wonder: "we were connected to things we could scarcely imagine."

— Sharona Muir, author of *Invisible Beasts*

Wendell Mayo's *Survival House* is middle-America on irradiated hallucinogens. In these remarkable and lyrical stories, we get to revel in Mayo's witty and sage blend of absurdist realism, and find, in the heartland of an America thoroughly marinated in the atomic age and a savage world history, characters so real and familiar they disarm us and convince us just how much we tend to live in denial. These entertaining stories get us, as the narrator of the title story puts it, "thinking about the sustainability of everything." Or anything. *Survival House* is, finally, insightful in the way all great fiction is: it delivers us to ourselves. Again.

— George Looney, author of *Meditations Before the Windows Fail* and *A Short Bestiary of Love and Madness*

Wendell's stories are confetti-blasted with historical nostalgia, and at the same time they flash a funhouse mirror up against our apocalypse-obsessed contemporary world. In *Survival House*, Wendell captures the horror of strangers—the watchers, the spies, the infiltrators—bubbling up from a McCarthyist tradition of paranoia. There isn't a writer who can better show us the absurdist nightmares and gut-busting humor of our own fears and doubts manifesting into monsters. And there couldn't be a more perfect time for a book like this in America. Through Wendell's rich prose and intricately developed characters, he reminds us of our humanity left seething behind the wake of nuclear annihilation.

— Dustin M. Hoffman, author of *One-Hundred-Knuckled Fist*

In this imaginative collection of subtly interwoven stories, master of short fiction Wendell Mayo showcases the absurdity, beauty and terror of post-industrial, pre-apocalyptic America. Iconic touchstones of atomic war, communist threat and even the Kennedy assassination are encountered here at street level by memorable characters, caught up between the "frightened alley cat" of history and "the precarious fortunes of enlightenment." Who else writing today so evocatively captures the familiar at its most bizarre, and the strange at its most familiar? Read *Survival House* and laugh, shudder, marvel.

—Cliff Hudder, author of *Splinterville* and *Pretty Enough for You*

Wendell Mayo's fiction is a lethal intoxicant that takes you on a mind-altering trip. You're hooked instantly and then the world never looks or feels the same. Here's the great fictional chronicler of the most exhilarating and spine-chilling period of American history: the decades of Cold War and the nuclear endgame, life on either side of the Iron Curtain. Miraculously, for all its other-worldliness, Mayo's disastrously funny stories remain fuzzy with honest small-town warmth—the flavor of that carnival hot dog and beer lingers long after you've shot out to Soviet Russia or the NASA space station and returned with psychedelic experiences to last a lifetime.

—Saikat Majumdar, author of *Play House*

ACKNOWLEDGMENTS

"The Big Healy" first appeared in *Lake Effect*; "Cherry Pie" in *Hotel Amerika*; "Commie Christmas" in *Christmas Stories from Ohio* (anthology); "Doom Town" in *Boulevard*; "A Kind of Tender Infinity" in *New Letters*; "Story of a Postcard" in *Chariton Review*; and "The World Is Ending Yesterday" in *Florida Review*.

The author is also grateful for the support of the Ohio Arts Council and the Fine Arts Work Center in Provincetown.

CONTENTS

DOOM TOWN

I have no dress except the one I wear every day.

-Madame Curie

Longest day of the year breaks as Sighrus Heeving and I head toward Luckey in his pickup. Light streaks east in sheets reflected by a cottony mass of clouds that list starboard into the horizon like the *Arizona* into Pearl Harbor, that day of infamy. Back in the rusty truck bed, Corporal Pig bucks against his heavy wire cage, squealing in bursts that blend into a seamless sinus shriek, then exhaust themselves in the dew-laden Ohio air. I try to bury the sound, focus on the steering wheel jiggling in Sighrus's hands, front-end sorely out of alignment. On the seat, the red bulls-eye of a Target shopping bag vibrates against his right hip.

"Simon," he says, nodding back at the riotous swine. "When we get in town, you mind the pig."

"Why do I have to mind the pig?"

"New guy in town always minds the pig," he says.

I glance at him, try to convince myself the man driving is not Sighrus, but now in costume, disguised as Robert Oppenheimer, Manhattan Project mastermind, his ratty tweed jacket, pale green tie twisted to one side in a farmer's knot, a dusty, mildew-gray Stetson cocked slightly left, and a candy cigarette with a bright pink tip dangling from his lower lip. But then I see his hook nose, charcoal Grecian Formula hair, mole on his right cheek dabbed with Cover Girl, and it's hard to imagine him anyone other than Sighrus Heeving, our Postmaster, who's retiring when they close our post office in a year or so and tuck our 399-citizen town into a wrinkle on a map, invisible.

I jack my legs onto the seat, twist a little left, and peer through the manure-smeared window at Corporal Pig, a big White Yorkshire dressed in fig-green Army fatigues, modified with Velcro strips to fit, the tick-thrack still in memory when, earlier that morning, I drove my shoulder into the pig, held him, while Sighrus-cum-Oppenheimer fitted the creature with the fatigues and explained with wallow-induced wheezing:

"In the 1950s, my father—"

"You mean Sighrus Senior, right?"

"Yes, while *my old man* was stationed at the Nevada Nuclear Test Site, his company was ordered to dress 1,200 Yorkshire pigs in Army duds and install them near Ground Zero in a barracks called The Pig Pen. Dad called it a Weapons Effect Test. Blooey! Talk about liking your bacon crisp."

I crack the pickup's window, let a little summer air run against my face.

"So that's all?" I ask Oppenheimer. "Mind the pig?"

"Of course. Corporal Pig's the guest of honor at Doom Town Festival."

Corporal Pig rolls an eyeball back a little, regards me suspiciously. Through his Army fatigues, I can see the outline of the big male's soccer-sized balls, the sort I once saw as a kid at the county fair fucking some sow senseless. Back then, I couldn't watch something like that long. The sheer explosion of procreative forces. Still can't.

I shudder, turn away as we squeal past Luckey's town limits sign. Someone's duct-taped cheap poster board over the sign, then hand-written on it.

DOOM TOWN
Pop. Zero

Behind the sign, three grain silos tower over Luckey, one retrofitted to dry red winter wheat, a crop some think will save the town after the crappy corn crop last fall. Someone's started the drier fans. The engines rev, moan low.

Oppenheimer pulls up to the old red-brick Post Office, "1925" chiseled into a cornerstone. He grabs his Target bag, gets out, goes around back, throws down the tailgate, laughs. I'm not only the new guy, but the younger guy as well, better fit, so Oppenheimer says, to retrieve the pig from the cage. He unlatches the cage door, then shoves me at the bed of the pickup and the Yorkshire, who's now outside the cage, headed for the tailgate.

"Just square up to him," Oppenheimer says. "Broadside."

"Right," I say, but somehow feel like that sow I saw at the Fair.

I scrabble over the tailgate and lurch at Corporal Pig. He backpedals.

"Hit him like you're gonna split that big boy." Oppenheimer whoops, flails his arms like a rodeo clown, and hops into the bed with me. "Like you're some bad-ass neutron!"

I lunge, drive my shoulder into the pig, seize him high on his torso. A dazzling mixture of operatic baritone grunts and soprano squeals issue from his jowls. His eyes roll back. I swear an instant they're locked onto mine, like this is more than a physical duel, like I'm in the presence of some preternatural intelligence beneath the boiling dust of dried mud roiling up from his spine, the scent of pig-shit, ammonia, and some other underlying odor. Rancid orange peels?

"Give me a nanosecond," Oppenheimer says, goes into his Target shopping bag, removes a large harness with a studded collar and leash. He slips the collar over the pig's head. With the straps, he circumnavigates the pig, back to belly to back, then buckles and snugs the harness tight against his father's fatigues.

He hands the leash to me.

I'm panting, covered with pig-filth, elbows to knees. The pig races back into the truck bed and proceeds to rake himself—and his Army uniform—against the sides.

"Motherfucker!" I say, hop down out the bed, and haul back on the leash until the pig scrambles off the tailgate.

I kick Corporal Pig a couple times to get him to stop straining at the leash.

"Hey," Oppenheimer warns, "you may not like that pig," he huffs, "but you damn well better…"

"I know," I say, "respect the uniform."

The *uniform*—the phrase catches Maude Roller's attention. She rises from her high-back rocker near the Post Office and trudges to the pickup wearing a black, Victorian, ankle-length dress. She tugs at the high collar crowding her thin neckline. Silver hair erupts from her forehead in an elliptical spray that resembles an electron cloud. In a slice of shade, her eyes glow a faint green, I suspect from special contact lenses. Pink rims her verdant orbs, making her sockets seem too large, like she's been crying. A lot. Many years ago, Maude moved from Cleveland to Luckey for its small-town charm. Now, I can't help think she's been crying about losing her job teaching fifth grade when the elementary school closed last month. She's only two years to retirement.

"Nice job with the eyes," Oppenheimer tells her. "And you are?"

"Madame Curie," she says. "I study radioactivity." She fixes her green gaze on me, like I'm an aberrant wave in a sea of calm. "And you are?"

"I mind the pig," I reply.

Then Sighrus launches into how he's Robert Oppenheimer, concluding with, "Madame, I've been practicing."

"Right," Madame says, leans back, and crushes her black bustle against the wheel-well of the pickup. She crosses her arms with calculated skepticism.

"I am become Death," Oppenheimer booms, "destroyer of worlds!"

As soon as he utters the dolorous words, his candy cigarette slips from his lip to the pavement and rolls into a sewer grating.

"Some destroyer," Madame mumbles. "Alright, Doctor Oppenheimer, you're so smart, what's smaller than the new subatomic God Particle they discovered?"

Oppenheimer hikes his Stetson a bit and scratches above one ear.

"Alright, what?" he says.

"My savings account."

Madame makes a tight little arc in the air with the tip of her nose, turns, and crosses the street to The Peachy Keen Hair Salon. The proprietor's Nessie Heeving, Sighrus's wife, who's recently discounted cuts from fifteen to five dollars, a move made to the acclaim of locals, who've now fashioned a handwritten sign taped to the front door.

THE BEST LITTLE HAIRHOUSE IN DOOM TOWN

Through the Hairhouse window, I see Nessie teasing Madame's cloud of hair into even more distant swirls of apogee and perigee. When I lug the pig across Main Street to get a closer look, I see Nessie wears a white prison smock, with ETHEL ROSENBERG embroidered on the right breast pocket. Her hair's pulled back in close, black curls that highlight her round face, rather like dark solar flares against a blank white sun. As Ethel works on Madame's hair, the tip of her tongue shows out one corner of her small mouth. Ethel seems placid, smiling patiently, as if she has no idea that, back in the fifties, Sing Sing Prison officials will need three separate jolts of electricity to kill her for spying for the Soviet Union, just minutes before the Jewish Sabbath begins.

A little uptown, I see Oppenheimer disappear into a corrugated steel maintenance shed behind the Sunoco station. I hear him banging about.

I yank Corporal Pig away from a squashed orange ice cream pushup on the sidewalk covered with blue bottle flies. We stroll over to the shed and stand in the open door. In the darkness I see Oppenheimer pushing a wheelbarrow, looking like it's full of tree limbs, but when he passes me and comes into light, I see there are three mannequins in the wheelbarrow, a male and female, face-up, and a child, face-down, all limbs akimbo.

"Need a hand?" I say, thinking I can tie Corporal Pig somewhere, or pawn him off on someone else.

"I got this," Oppenheimer replies.

He pushes the load back to the Post Office, where he removes a mannequin, a male, and positions it on the steel bench. He takes the female and the child across the street, where Madame waits with a baby carriage. She stations the female and child behind the carriage, bent slightly, looking at what I can only assume is a happy infant inside. Oppenheimer shuttles more mannequins from the shed to Main Street. When a man pulls up with a 1953 Hudson Super Jet, mint green, beautifully restored, he gets out and Oppenheimer installs a mannequin behind the steering wheel. A man at the Sunoco drags a fifties' Dr. Pepper chest cooler out the front door and sets it in front of the station. Oppenheimer places a mannequin, bent at the waist, to retrieve a cool drink. Women and children, I mean flesh and blood ones, soon crowd the downtown, dressing mannequins in brown Fedoras, blue pleated pants, green double-breasted rayon shirts, violet calico dresses, bonnets with broad yellow brims that seem to glow in the early morning sun. More vintage cars roll in and park at curbs. Corporal Pig and I stroll over to inspect each old car: a cherry-red Nash Rambler, deep purple Desoto Diplomat, and a glossy blue Ford job called a Meteor. The town transforms, the way Oppenheimer puts it his last trip with the mannequins, "as if life suddenly switches from black-and-white to color the way it happens in *The Wizard of Oz.*"

While the pig and I go over to fuss about the mannequins' attire, fasten an errant button, adjust a wig, smooth a pleat, a kid sets up to sell lemonade in front of the Hairhouse. I go for a glass.

"Little man," I say to the red-haired kid with matching freckles. "How about watching my pig awhile?"

"No way, mister," he says smiling with as much capacity as his face will furnish. "Hey," he adds, "you must be the new guy."

I give the kid his nickel, enjoy my lemonade, then see, through the thick bottom of the glass, Corporal Pig staring up at me. Just staring, for pigs don't pant, sweat, anything. He just looks thirsty with that weird intelligence I noticed wrestling him out of Oppenheimer's pickup. I'm thinking I've taken this animal from its rightful wallow and I'm to mind him. And Army fatigues can't make the pig any less dehydrated.

"Alright!" I say to Corporal Pig's pleading eyes, get another glass of lemonade, and set it in front of him. The pig laps the lemonade awhile, then tips and breaks the kid's glass on the sidewalk. I kick the glass shards away from the pig. Lemonade Kid starts crying "My mom's gonna kill me!" so I give him a dollar to shut him up, all the while the pig's rasping his tongue against the concrete to absorb the last molecule of lemonade.

A fireman in full fifties gear and smoke mask stops over with a wrench and cracks the valve of a hydrant. Corporal Pig drinks from the rusty stream, then stands in the brown gush and soaks himself. I'm about to ask the fireman if he'll mind looking after the pig awhile, when the pig begins to nosedive into mud formed by firewater, ready to wallow. I drag him by his leash back to the Post Office, where a dozen members of the Salvation Army in red coats and plumed hats gather with musical instruments, tuning them wildly in the mid-morning humidity. An old black Cadillac, top down, the sort Kennedy was killed in, pulls around the musicians. An elderly woman stands in it, platinum-blonde, in a nude body stocking over which a cloud of cotton wads adhere to her pelvis, belly, and breasts, in total shaped like a mushroom cloud. She's thick with makeup and lipstick applied beyond the lines, like Carol Channing in *Hello, Dolly!* When I glance her way she smiles cheesecake at me, like an explosion of personality, then shoots her arms skyward and says, "Whoosh!"

Loose muscle flaps beneath her withered biceps. A silver sash divides her body.

MISS ATOMIC BOMB 1957

Over kids' giggles and adult groans, Miss Atomic Bomb repeats. "Whoosh!"

Less like an atomic explosion and more a kind of badly acted death gasp, a last leukemic rattle in the chest.

She startles the pig.

She's got to be in her seventies.

Oppenheimer arrives, speaks with the Salvation Army Band leader, then shakes his head in disappointment. I hear a few of the band members break into "Deck the Halls," while the grain drier whistles in accompaniment. Red wheat dust flies about town like a crimson snow squall.

"Jesus," Oppenheimer says, coming up to me fast. "It's all they'll play. Christmas stuff."

He takes me squarely by the shoulders, steers Corporal Pig and me to the very head of the Doom Town parade.

"You really want me *here*?" I ask Oppenheimer but get no answer.

At first, I feel really alone at the head of the parade. Kids and parents line the street. When I glance behind, Miss Atomic Bomb blows me a greasy red kiss. The band director smiles at me. Several rows of heads bob behind them.

Soon, Gus Gobbelnec arrives, a dairy farmer forced to sell his place to MegaMilk Corporation. He's in Bermuda shorts and his chicken legs scarcely seem to support two large cardboard cutouts suspended from his shoulders with brown twine. Each cutout is shaped like an atomic bomb, dark, elliptical in aspect, fixed with four stabilizing fins. I see hand-lettered on each side:

FAT MAN
21 kilotons

Madame runs up and starts kicking Fat Man hard in his scrawny exposed ankles.

"Fat Man? Really?" she says and glares at Oppenheimer, who shrugs. "He wants to dress like that *Bomb* this year?" She reaches up to adjust a black hairclip that wobbles on her head with each syllable. "I thought we agreed. No reminders of Nagasaki—or Hiroshima!"

Fat Man goes to his knees while our town cop, wearing a Harry Truman mask, pulls Madame off Fat Man. Truman removes Fat Man's signs from his shoulders and sets them inside the Sunoco, leaving a frowning Fat Man clad only in his Bermudas heading for the back of the parade.

Madame walks up, beaming, and stands on my right. Oppenheimer settles in on my left. The band begins with "O Little Town of Bethlehem." Oppenheimer jabs me in the ribs. Miss Atomic Bomb starts whooshing. I swipe tiny red balls of wheat dust from my forehead, tug at Corporal Pig's leash, and we head off Main down Church Street, so named because of the church that has stood there since 1885. Grass around the church is high, gone to seed. A satellite dish pokes out one side smothered in a briar bush. The church itself, all of it, from base to steeple and cross, is painted a ridiculously inoffensive beige. Planted squarely in the tree lawn is a sign.

CHAIN REACTION REALTY, INC.
SHORT SALE
GET CLOSER TO GOD IN THIS CHARMING FIXER-UPPER!

"The church failed last year," Madame says to me.

"How's a church fail?" I ask.

"Beats me," she shrugs.

I stop walking, agog at the church. Corporal Pig stops. Madame stops. Oppenheimer stops. Band stops playing. Everyone stops. The town's silent, except for the sound of the grain driers whistling and red particulates drifting through air.

Oppenheimer and Madame both look at me with a kind of obedient impatience.

"Whenever you're ready," Oppenheimer says.

"Me?"

"All at your pace," Madame says.

I walk forward, jerk the pig with me, realize that pig and I not only head the parade, but lead it. A couple times I test the parade. I stop, stoop, pat Corporal Pig on the head. Music stops. Everyone stops. Then I walk. Music starts, people walk, Miss Atomic Bomb's whooshing again. I hate minding the pig, but like how it comes with the power to stop and start the parade. It's one of those quantum moments, millisecond events you think might change your life forever, like when Sharon accused me of having an obsessive need for approval.

Day of signing our separation papers, I told Sharon, "I'm thinking of putting my English degree to work, applying for a position at Winky's Café. What do you think?"

"See?" she said. "You're doing it again!"

I suppose she was right.

But I wish she could see me now, my absolute power over the Doom Town Parade.

We turn right onto Liberty Hi Street, pass boarded-up Epic Elementary, and follow the irrigation ditch dotted with empty bottles, cans, and wild orange lilies. We surge past Dead People's Stuff, a windowed storeroom of unpacked antiques, behind a glass door and sign that reads, "Here When Here." We march by The Temple of Groom, Wolf Man's doggie salon, defunct since his paralyzed sister passed and he again pursues his dream of running the Iditarod. Finally, we pass Many Happy Returns, tax preparation while you wait, abandoned, renovated by a CPA's mother to lure him back home, though she hasn't heard a word from him since he took a job with some big financial group in New York shortly before the economy tanked in 2008. No one's heard from him since.

When we turn right onto Perry Street, the band breaks into "Silent Night."

Around noon, the pig and I halt at the Post Office.

I glance at Oppenheimer.

"Cool parade," I tell him. "Now, what do I do with the pig?"

"Hang on," he tells me, then turns and faces parade-goers. "Good job, everyone!"

I'm tied to this animal for hours and all he can say is hang on?

People scatter, talking, laughing. Kids run to the far end of Main Street, a little past the Sunoco, where a couple carnies assemble a Ferris wheel and merry-go-round. A man in a yellow radiation suit chases a couple screaming kids with his Geiger counter. Corporal Pig pulls me over to the curb near the Hairhouse, where a hot dog truck's now parked. It's near noon and I'm hungry. I feel like congratulating myself for leading the parade, so I get the biggest dog, the Buster-Jangle. I'm in the process of stuffing the sweating dog in my mouth for bite one, when, again, I catch Corporal Pig's eyes—hungry ones. I tear off a chunk of my dog and kneel to feed it to my companion. He just about has his snoot and mouth around the morsel, when I withdraw the dog, think how there're all kinds of meat products in there, how maybe feeding Corporal Pig this dog may be tantamount to cannibalism. I remove the forbidden meat from the bun and toss the bread to him. He shovels it along the sidewalk with his snout before it disappears in his mouth.

Before I can complete my meal of the naked dog, Oppenheimer comes up. He takes me by the elbow and guides me and Corporal Pig to the center of the street opposite the Post Office.

"Okay," he says, "it's time."

"Time?" I say.

"Just mind the pig," he says, "a little longer."

I see everyone half-running indoors. Mothers and fathers hustle children into the Sunoco, Hairhouse, Post Office, any nearest building on Main Street.

Miss Atomic Bomb hobbles over to me and Corporal Pig.

"I'm really sorry," she whispers, but before she can finish

Oppenheimer has her by her cotton waist and shoves her inside the Post Office.

It's just me and Corporal Pig. Alone. On Main Street. By now the grain drier's shrill like a jet turbine. Bits of red dust flit about our heads. I'm aware of the mannequins about me, amazed by the short length of time it takes for one to be alone around inanimate objects before you feel like one. I'm the plastic mother, frozen in time, gazing in on her child. I'm the immobile man, hands folded on chest, resting on the bench by the Hairhouse. I'm the dead-tired man standing by his Hudson Super Jet after a long day at the office.

I'm Every-Mannequin.

A siren blasts from the top of the grain drier, same civil defense wail one hears in old movies to warn of an impending atom-bomb attack, the sort of sound that saturates the air so thoroughly that any possibility of echo within the sound vanishes. Corporal Pig shivers at the end of his leash. His jowls bounce as if he's squealing, but I can't hear anything except the siren. I'm looking inside buildings, trying to find a human face, but can't. Part of me waits for the atomic detonation, another tells me how silly it is to think it may happen. I'm getting angry, feel duped, want to rush indoors and give them all hell for making me part of this ridiculous charade. But if I run, they'll think I'm frightened by their stupid siren. If I stay, they'll think I go along with them in their dumb Doom Town game. So I don't do anything. I stand, middle of Main Street, paralyzed, red dust settling in my hair. The pig and I stand alone, most alone, the big alone.

When the siren stops, townspeople come out into the street, but a few adults remain inside to mind the children. Oppenheimer appears, walks up, puts his arm around me. He claps my shoulder and draws me close to his side.

He raises one arm and addresses the people of Doom Town.

"Yeah, over to Whitehouse they got their fuckin Cherry Festival," he says. "Other towns celebrate radishes, watermelons, apple butter. How fuckin touching. But not Doom Town. We're the mother of all festivals. We celebrate the survival of the entire human-fuckin-race!"

The townspeople instantly applaud and Oppenheimer turns to me.

"Welcome to Doom Town!" he shouts.

He snatches Corporal Pig's leash from my hand.

"So," I say, "I'm not to mind the pig anymore?"

"Of course not," he whispers. "You're one of us, kid!" he booms out to the crowd, then adds, "Now, let's eat!"

DOOM TOWN

He guides Corporal Pig behind the Sunoco station, where I can see a couple men digging a pit. I walk a little that way, see the pig, Oppenheimer pull a pistol, hear it crack twice, then see the pig fall, legs kicking the way the body doesn't know the brain is dead for quite some time. A few Doomtowners wince. Then I hear the distant tick-thrack of Oppenheimer separating the Velcro and removing his father's Army uniform from the pig's body.

Children return to the street. Madame comes up to me.

"I know that pig dies for us all," she says. "Symbolic, I suppose. But I'm glad it's over."

"And me?" I ask. "What am I supposed to symbolize?"

"You?" She reaches up and pats an electric mass of her hair that snaps in the humidity. "You minded the pig."

Near dusk, carnies have the rides going and the air is laced with the scent of charcoal and kerosene, a haze of smoke over the pit behind the Sunoco. A beer vendor sets up. They make me get a plastic wristband to show I'm old enough to drink. Beer flows. People get friendlier. Oppenheimer's bombed. He's eaten all his candy cigarettes and chain smokes the real deal. His Stetson's on backward, hiked high on his head.

A couple kids arrange two mannequins to have mission-style sex on the bench near the Hairhouse. Poor guy on top, his pants are tugged low, plastic ass-crack showing. Madame runs over, takes a swipe at one kid, then nervously sets the lascivious pair back to rights. Another kid sells canned food with photoshopped skulls and crossbones on them saying "Irradiated—Consume At Own Risk!" I ask the kid why anyone would buy such a thing, then that moment someone does, and the kid says, eyes surprised, "It's just cool, mister."

By nightfall, I'm beer-numbed, grinning like an idiot. I watch lights of carnival rides. Lights in the darkness. Light everywhere, whirling, spinning, dancing, children delighting in it. So much light. But when rides shut down, Main Street is lit only by a handful of tiki lamps. In the frail light I see Ethel Rosenberg through the Hairhouse window, sitting in her salon chair, shouting something at Robert Oppenheimer, the tail end of which sounds like "I don't even know you!" Oppenheimer storms into the street, elbows his way through a small crowd, and staggers over, reeking of beer and cigarettes.

He claps an arm each about Madame and me.

"We're all sons of bitches now," he says. "Aren't we?"

"Give it a rest, Sighrus," Madame replies and wriggles free of him.

"Screw you, Maude," he says.

Oppenheimer removes his Stetson, tosses it to Lemonade Kid, then spits his glowing cigarette to the ground. Madame Curie takes her hair down and unfastens the top three buttons of her black dress. I watch an older kid sneak up on Miss Atomic Bomb and snatch a large wad of cotton from her left breast. She's all out of whoosh, sits in a rocker that knocks against the Post Office windowsill, and smears lipstick onto a paper towel. More people begin to drop their disguises. I get to know Enrico Fermi, who discourses on the dangers of chemical lawn treatments while putting away a sugar-dusted funnel cake; then Albert Einstein, who's got cats, too many, and explains how you know a cat's happy when it blinks at you with both eyes, who wishes it were as easy to tell with people; and then Senator Joe McCarthy who, finding out I've an English degree, wants me to read his novel-in-progress concerning his impossibly expensive hip replacement surgery. Townspeople mill about in dim flickering light. Shadows of their aliases dance wildly, grow tall on the old brick of the Post Office, so tall the shadows seem their greater disguises, indistinguishable from those mannequins cast.

Madame-cum-Maude comes over, leans in close. In darkness, her head seems to float above her unseen black dress, green-fire eyes still ablaze.

"Back then," she says, "they chose Yorkshire pigs to test in atomic blasts because their flesh most resembles human flesh."

When she leaves, I'm alone. I listen a lot, hear "human-fuckin-race" drift through the air a couple times, then, "you'll see, things'll come around." All the while, shadows continue to dance about me. So many blithe shadows. I'm guessing these are hard times in Luckey, but tonight, just tonight, in Doom Town there's plenty of Corporal Pig to go around. Me, I'm nobody, wasted, by now working on my second helping, listening as more shadows talk of red winter wheat and of autumn corn. They talk of a bonfire, of the Sun King embracing the Queen of Summer. They talk of getting more beer, of staying up all night to greet the dawn, of waiting for something to change, of one almighty moment that saves every-damn-one.

THE TRANS-SIBERIAN RAILWAY COMES TO WHITEHOUSE

Herbie and I were out back of the Train Wreck Tavern, sky spread with late-summer stars, Herbie stooped over the eyepiece of his telescope, searching the Moon's craggy face for something to save his bar, any scrap of inspiration in crisp, unclouded shadows of a crater or lunar mountain range. Some cosmic connection. Anything to bring people back to the Train Wreck.

"There's a sign up there," he said, then unstuck his eyeball from the focal tube of the telescope. "I know it."

We went back inside, took our stools at the empty bar. Herbie pulled on his Iron City brew, sudzed his nose, winced from the beer sting, and wiped the foam with the back of a hand. He grabbed his cell off the bar and started googling ideas.

"Here's one," he said. "Hospital night, when you can be hand-fed by nurses, and for a five-dollar upcharge you can get fed wearing a strait jacket."

I stared at him.

"Why not?" he said.

I informed him that Whitehouse was a bastion of retirees, or soon-to-bes, and may not appreciate that little peek at their futures, my own closer than I wanted to admit after my forced retirement from Euler's Feed and Grain.

But it wasn't for want of imagination that Herbie was a failure. The usual appeal to Saturday club bikers ended when a genuine 24/7 biker drove his Indian into the Train Wreck, dropped the kickstand, and left it running, a blue cloud that cleared the place in seconds. Herbie tried Zombie Night Tuesdays to appeal to younger people, but even our most broad-minded youth still minded scabs of latex in their chicken noodle soup and burgers lacerated the color of bruise-wheel makeup—and Zombie Night service was slow, really S-L-O-W.

Anyway, staring at the Moon for a connection must've been what got Herbie thinking that Friday at euchre. I had his wife, Ana, as my partner, leaving Herbie with Pearl, who made some wisecrack about how we were wife swapping until Ana made a wild-eyed squint and began to hold forth about how her grandmother told her she was the illegitimate issue—and she used the word 'issue'—of Leon Trotsky.

"Bronstein," I said, trying to show off my degree in history, which was of no use during my thirty-five years at the Feed and Grain.

"Trotsky, Bronstein, whatever," Ana said and went on: "My great-grandmother was a maid aboard the steamship *Montserrat* out of Barcelona, Christmas Day, 1916. She was from Luxembourg and told my grandmother how the thick-browed Bolshevik impregnated her in his stateroom while Natalya and his boys were above deck enjoying the views of Valencia and Malaga. He was fucking great-grandma doggie style against the valet while discoursing on the 'dictatorship of the working class,' how we can all be dictators, like, together. Then he came in her. When she turned around to see what was next, he looked puzzled, limp-dicked, and said to her, 'Come to think of it, you are the only one who does any work on this capitalist rust-bucket.' He paused to zip his trousers with one final tug. 'So, I guess you're in charge.'"

Herbie, Ana's husband for decades, believing himself to know her deepest secrets, was wide-eyed. Me, I trumped Ana's ace which left her, now, in my estimation, with a revolutionary scowl.

"Trotsky?" Herbie squeaked. "Really? Your grandmother was one of the deluded masses, that's all."

"Not funny," I said and tried to shuffle cards Vegas-style for the next hand. A few leapt from the deck into my lap.

"I read his biography," Ana said. "I'm like him: bright blue eyes, terrified of snakes, as a kid prone to blacking out and pissing the floor, and you know how I can blow perfect cigarette smoke rings."

"Trotsky?" Herbie repeated.

"Perfect rings," Ana whispered.

Herbie's hands dropped to his lap.

"I can't believe," I said, "that smoke rings seal the deal. There isn't a connection. Herb? Herbie!"

THE TRANS-SIBERIAN RAILWAY COMES TO WHITEHOUSE

But why not? In our little Whitehouse where no connection may exist, we made one, going back as far as Watergate in the 70s, when our mayor, one of a dynasty of Republican leaders, had a top-rate security system installed in his home, which also served as his campaign headquarters, compliments of taxpayers, "Just to be sure there's no funny business here in this Whitehouse."

Still, I interjected again.

"Smoke rings?"

And then Herbie reminded me how Gus Gobbelnec had googled satellite shots of our fair borough, and discovered that blocks of homes formed the toothy grin of the Cheshire Cat. When Bill Ruhe took his crop duster up one night and returned with pictures, one could see lights from our homes form the enigmatic Cheshire's smile. According to Herbie, we were connected to things we could scarcely imagine. Had to be.

"Why not?" he asked us.

Too bad more people don't actually try to answer 'why not?' these days. So it was too late.

"Trotsky. Russia." Herbie's face was awash with an Archimedean paradigm shift. "That's it!"

And so Herbie made sure word got around Whitehouse how Ana was a genuine dyed-in-the-blood commie, a Trotsky, no less than the People's Commissar of Military and Naval Affairs after the October Revolution, and was thinking about such and such a theme for the Train Wreck, and folks around Whitehouse said, "Why not?" And no one tried to answer it then, either.

The Railway arrived at the Train Wreck in late fall, in pieces, with a construction crew of three illegals, who built the platform and set G-gauge tracks upon which the model train and flat cars snaked from kitchen to dining room, such that the route touched every red-white-and-blue plaid tabletop, then wound its way behind the bar and back to the kitchen.

I was on my third Iron City when Herbie came into the bar, festooned a couple windows with red-and-white crepe paper, then scotch-taped an ink-jet banner where the train exited the kitchen:

THE WHITEHOUSE TRANS-SIBERIAN RAILWAY

I sat, drinking to my reflection in the mirror behind the bar, bemusing a beer ad, a menacing red neon shark fin sticking out a glowing yellow wave.

Herbie came to my side, shoved a new, laminated menu my way, and pushed my unfinished Iron City aside. I retrieved my brew and tilted the menu into a narrow shaft of reddish yellow light from the beer ad behind the bar.

УБЕЖИЩЕ Троцкого
Supreme Soviet Dining

Herbie bent one ear of the menu right, then beamed.

"I googled the first part." He ran a fingertip slowly over the Cyrillic, proudly announcing:

TROTSKY'S HIDEAWAY

"I'm not surprised," I said and Herbie let the corner of the menu snap back.

I read on in the menu, had underestimated Herbie's utilitarian genius. There they were, a rogue's gallery of repasts:

THE KHRUSHCHEV

A generous mound of sauerkraut concealing missile-shaped sausages, all swimming in blue mashed potatoes.

THE GORBACHEV

Prime beef on one side. Hot gravy on the other side. Both divided by a thick wall of mashed potatoes. Tear down this wall!

THE PUTIN

Appears to be an all-American hamburger, but conceals a layer of dark Beluga sturgeon eggs slathered on the burger. Also called 'The Volga.' For the hardcore Trotsky's lover.

On a special Pork Page, various smiling faces of Orwellian pigs decorated the margins, dishes ready for end-consumption by Trotsky's patrons: the Napoleon, the Snowball, and the Squealer. Seniors could order The Old Major, kids, the Minimus.

Trotsky's grand opening, men, women, and children lined up at the bar, paid ten bucks apiece, and were directed to sit at a certain table.

The train rolled out the kitchen for the first time, a locomotive and three flatcars each fitted with a metal tray loaded with a heaping Gorbachev. Middle America loved mashed potatoes. It first stopped at the table occupied by Ana and my Pearl, then at the Gobbelnecs'. Gus prodded his mighty wall while his wife Ester and their kids watched with jaw-dropping wonder. The train chugged away, headed for the kitchen, smoke from special pellets puffing, leaving a smell linger like burnt hair stuck on the glow element of a cheap hairdryer. Then a familial squeal arose from the Gobbelnecs' table as the potato wall finally gave and gravy met meat for the first time.

Only once that opening day did anyone question the new menu. Gus told Herbie he suspected his generous block of mashed-Berlin Wall was made of instant potatoes. Within minutes, Herbie countered the propaganda, writing on the grease board in the front entrance:

"Remember, comrades, quantity has a quality all its own!—Joseph Stalin."

After a time, a miniature air raid siren sounded, Kids pasted palms to ears. Parents smiled painfully. Then the train came around to take dirty dishes back into the kitchen. On a grease board in the entryway, Herbie'd scrawled, "Buss your own tables; or you may be exiled from Trotsky's, as Comrade Stalin says, 'No man—no problem.'"

The Railway was a model of collectivized efficiency.

Of course, no one was actually ejected, but for offenders, of which there were few, Herbie'd hired a retired priest to wash dishes. Time to time, he'd come quietly into the dining room and use the hook at one end of his cane like a pastoral staff to gaff dirtied dishes.

We called him the Bishop.

"How's the Bishop in atheist Russia authentic, Herb?" I asked.

"Of course, he's authentic. In Trotsky's, everyone has something to hide," Herbie said. "I bet you have something to hide." He set a bottle of Stoli on the bar. "I'm watching you."

I thought I could take it. Hiding? What could I be hiding? Who could hide anything these days? I thought about globalization, worldliness, otherliness, multi-everything all over at once, like a sour mash of humanity, the mess of it all, and for a moment I felt it, no secrets, whatever they were, shoulder-to-shoulder with everyone on the entire planet, even Reds of older times. What a brew!—and buzzed, to boot. I checked my watch, eight p.m., stewed right on schedule.

Herbie nodded at my Iron City, then tapped the side of the bottle of Stoli.

"That's all I'm serving from now on."

Stoli. The word sounded like a rifle shot. I couldn't believe it. I clutched my Iron City, precious little of the brew left, coddled it like a fluid gold ingot.

"What do you mean by all this commie crap!" I shouted, alarming my Pearl who was smack in the midst of destroying her mashed potato wall. "Herbie, it's communism."

"At least it ain't socialism," Herbie replied. I gave him an astonished, inebriant stare. "You know. *Socia*lism. Big government. Washington. Duh. Remember? At least I ain't outsourcing democracy. I'm insourcing communism. Keeping jobs here. Why not?"

Why not? That question again. I seemed a slave to the silence following his pronouncement. He nodded at me with a kind of shrewd knowledge and comradery any commie would be proud of, and I mean he glowed, like the red fin of the neon shark that framed our two hunched outlines at the bar in the celebrious gloaming.

After closing, the three men who'd installed the Railway took sides of Herbie's pool table and began to inch it out the bar. I ran to its side.

"Leave it a minute, okay?" I pleaded.

Herbie shook his head, watching me in the mirror behind the bar. I ran a hand over the pool table, its wrinkled, beer-stained, threadbare felt. I stared lovingly at the resulting sticky blue chalk dust on my hand. I stooped, let my hand fall, and caressed the thick curvaceous table legs, each foot an enormous eagle's claw gripping a ball. I closed my eyes, reached a little higher, and placed my fingertips gently on the raised surfaces of the plastic nameplate.

GOOD QUALITY AND CHEAP POOL TABLE
Made in Guangzhou, China

Feeling each letter made me feel its impending loss even more keenly, recalling the repeated and varied sentiments that the nameplate brought out in times before the Siberian Railway arrived:

"Not bad for a pool table made in fucking China," I'd say to Herbie.

"Yeah," he'd say, "but it's got American balls—and that's what matters."

I nodded to one of the men. He hung his head in commiserative silence, then waved the other men to continue carrying the pool table out.

I dragged my feet back to Herbie at the bar.

"I hope you're happy," I said to him, finding his eyes in the mirror. "That's the last shred of what's American in this joint."

Herbie gazed prophetically at the Trans-Siberian Railway.

"I gotta have authenticity in Trotsky's," he said. "That's what's in short supply. That's what's in demand. Profit. That's the bottom line."

"Thank God for your wife's ass," I said to Herbie.

We were in Herbie's place in parkas, watching vapor clouds rise from our nostrils and vanish above our heads. The marquee, TROTSKY'S HIDEAWAY, had just gone up outside. We waited for the dinner rush, finishing a last six-pack of Iron City, atop barstools recently warmed by our wives' asses, Ana's, where my derriere was parked, and Pearl's, where Herbie's rump rested.

Herbie wriggled his butt a bit in the transient warmth of the pleather barstool.

He grinned.

"Thanks for your wife's ass as well."

It didn't humor me much. I was in a dark mood, staring at row after row of Stoli bottles covering the entire liquor case behind the bar, a la Warhol.

I watched our wives stumble out the front door of "Trot's" as locals now called it, into the stunning January Ohio sunlight, warm by sight, bitter cold by feel.

"Do you have to keep this fucking place so cold?" I asked.

"Tuesdays are Parka Night. Saves money," he replied, "and makes the whole experience more real."

By real, he meant customers were expected to appreciate a piping-hot Khrushchev, Gorbachev, or Putin in the frigid environs of Herbie's Siberia. If you didn't bring your own sub-zero parka, Herbie had several he loaned customers.

Parka Night was packed. The Trans-Siberian Railway that delivered Trotsky's fare now moved through a synthetic snow-covered hilly landscape dotted with plastic fir and pine, and stopped at a quaint, miniature station with a sign above:

ŠALČININKAI

"Cold Land," Herbie translated, "in Lithuanian. A clearinghouse for deportees from the Baltics and Eastern Europe. Gus Gobbelnec told me about it."

Gobbelnec had also loaned Herbie Red Army soldiers from his Marx playset, *The Road to Stalingrad*, complete with wild-eyed Russian peasants in bearish burly papaka hats charging Nazis.

"*Marx* playset?" I said demurely.

"Yeah," Herbie replied, "Louis Marx, not Karl, but you wonder if there's a connection. Why not?"

Indeed.

I took one of the plastic peasants in my hand.

"Those aren't deportees," I said. "Not even close. Jesus. The Stalin regime murdered hundreds of thousands."

"Well," Herbie replied, deep in thought. "Marx didn't make a *Road to Siberia* playset, did he? And even if he had, how would a kid even play with that sort of thing?"

Some time passed, the interval of which I decided I hated Herbie and Trotsky's, not on ideological or historical grounds, but because, as I watched the last slips of Iron City drain back into my mug, I realized I was not buzzed enough, and there wasn't a drop of brew left in the place. I found myself wanting the Stoli back of the bar, only a few feet from my grasp. Stoli. The Russian repast represented everything I'd come to also hate as a kid. The duck and cover drills. My old man razing Mom's Victory Garden and scooping out an A-bomb shelter, which still existed last year, the day of his dying breath, his last words, "In case that prick Putin tries something."

I almost surrendered to the Stoli, when in walked Ana, or someone vaguely resembling her, parka velcroed at the neck, yet a seductive creature, with thick, long eyebrows, cerise lipstick on a mouth drawn taut in a high-chinned pout. Her hair, once gray, was now midnight black, parted severely down the middle, then braided into a thick black rope piled atop the part and pinned with a bone-colored shaft. Large hoop earrings hung from her earlobes, resembling snakes eating their tails.

"Frida-Fucking-Kahlo?" I said.

Herbie looked at Ana, whose shoulders-back Mexican pride gave way to a brief shrug.

"Well, anyway," Ana said, "I liked her picture in Trotsky's biography. And she was a commie."

And indeed our Ana was because people took her for one as she greeted patrons that evening, complete with their parkas, fog-breaths, and stiff Soviet smiles. Their rugged, hurt-like countenances seemed to forebear the cold in favor of Herbie's commie cuisine.

The Trans-Siberian Railway went round and round, dutifully delivering dishes prepared by Herbie's newly hired cook, no mere apparatchik like the Bishop, nicknamed "Rasputin," because of his unruly hair-netted beard and how he'd survived a beating, gunshot wound, and stabbing in a drug-buying attempt. His real name was Homer, Gus Gobbelnec's eldest son, recently enrolled in a culinary correspondence course affectionately called "Cooking with *Convict*-ion," seeing as it was part of his conditions for parole when he was released a few weeks before from the county lockup. No one really knew what Rasputin'd done to land him in the slammer. His dad wasn't talking, even when lit with Stoli, and when someone asked, Gus would mention some sort of global conspiracy or other, something sure to change the subject among citizens of Whitehouse.

One day, I stood, center of four impressions in the carpet, made by the lovely legs of my departed pool table. Herbie stood at my side saying something about getting a display and bust of Lenin to fill the space.

The long tongue of Herbie's measuring tape flitted out. He knelt, laid it on the carpet and made some measurements.

"I can't believe you hired Homer," I said.

"Rasputin," he corrected.

"Raspy Putin," I replied. "Whatever."

"It don't matter who you were before," he said. "Now, in Trotsky's, anyone might have a job here doing anything."

People seemed to like the food Rasputin served. Missile sausages shot up through The Khrushchev's secret mounds of sauerkraut to waiting mouths of freezing customers. Wall after wall of mashed went down, releasing flood-tides of gravy onto heaps of meat steaming in the frigid air. Gus Gobbelnec was trying The Putin and, with an acquiescent wince, put away two layers of sturgeon eggs, I suppose in honor of his convict-son's newfound calling.

Weeks passed, and Frida worked roses, begonias, and petunias into her rope-piled hairstack. People seemed to like her. When not exhibiting herself for customers, she spent time behind the bar at the mirror adjusting the hairstack. After a time, she penciled in the thin ghost-moustache of Frida's.

Herbie seemed transformed as well, his hair long, wild, flipped high, like a wave about to break that never does. He added *more* gray to his only-sixty-year old head, got coin-round bifocals, a gray sweater vest, tie, and shoddy woolen overcoat. For all the world, he looked like an aging Trotsky. But the bright blue contacts he popped into his eyes were the end of me. And he said *I* had something to hide!

I'd grown sick of drinking Iron City alone at home, no one to appreciate my special rhythm of tip and draught, of satisfied sigh, of a buzz long and coming on a fond, *warm* night in an American tavern.

I'd had it.

It was another Tuesday and Parka Night. I turned to Herbie, who sat next to me in his usual barstool, straightening his necktie in the egregious red funk of the neon shark fin.

"Really, Herb? Blue contacts?" I said with a menacing smile. "You do know Trotsky was assassinated, a hand axe planted in his cranium, right?"

"Yeah," he replied, swiping a hand over the hairy mess on his head, "things were more personal in those days."

He got this libidinous smile on his face that traveled the breath-fogged dining room to Frida's waiting Latin eyes. And I knew it. Knew it with the same certainty I'd come to know that Whitehouse, Ohio could very well be connected to all things worldly, and to ideas, and history, and current events, podcasts, every CNN blip-a-minute of every day. Whitehouse must matter to everyone in some strange and inexplicable way. The world's desires were ours.

I tapped old Herbie-cum-Trotsky on the shoulder. He turned to me and glanced down his spectacles, irritated.

"You and Ana—excuse me, I mean, Frida—are fucking again. Am I right?"

He smiled, returned his attention to the Latin object of his desire, and I knew it was so, after all the years of hearing him whine about his frigid wife.

I guess I wanted some of that in my own aging marriage, not Frida, but my own Pearl, whom I now imagined in deep, Siberian winter, I myself, Doctor Yuri Zhivago, making love to my Lara Antipov, alone in our silent icehouse of desire.

It was then, a moment of icehouse passion, that I did the unthinkable. I stumbled behind the bar, fetched a bottle of Stoli from the shelf, poured a shot, brought it trembling to my lips, and tipped it down, a fire racing along my esophagus, the Railway coasting by with a new batch of steaming Putins, my eyes advancing on Pearl, who was helping Frida with an errant bit of rope hair from the pile on her head. I crossed the room, took my Lara Antipov in my arms, dipped her low, tongue-kissed her in front of everyone, then collapsed with my new Russian beauty onto the floor, my knee replacement reminding me of my age.

"Ypa!"

The cry went up from the room, along with a number of shot glasses, clinking in the cold, along with like sounds from kids' glasses of Shirley Temples.

My Lara smiled, slowly drew herself to her knees, then feet, and hauled me by the hand out of Trotsky's, home, and to our bedroom.

That night the snow fell, thick and silent, and I was as content as I had ever been, early retirement or not.

In anticipation of Siberian spring, Herbie ended Tuesday Parka Nights. Business was good. People kept coming, and brought family and relatives. Herbie'd trained customers well. We scarcely saw the Bishop in the dining room to clear dishes. Eventually, Herbie hired a couple high school kids from nearby Tontogany to celebrate, taught them to dance a rudimentary hopak, dressed them suitably, and had them perform on weekends.

Whitehouse was transformed, no longer a place of retirees, pensioners, social security and disability checks, of old Crown Vics and pickups few could afford to repair. We were lovers, revolutionaries, toughened by winter, warmed by necessity in our hearts, passions that burned all the more because once a week all winter we'd been literally freezing in Trotsky's. Dead revolutionary Russia had breathed new life into Whitehouse.

A food critic from the *Luckey Whistler* weekly came in one night. It was Sighrus Heeving, looking for something to do when he retired from his job at the Post Office in Luckey. We were pleasantly surprised when his review, circulated to 819 homes hereabouts, concluded that Trotsky's was "Charming, with commie cheap eats, and a great example of American ingenuity and individualism."

We think it was Sighrus's comment about "American…individualism" that started all the trouble. The article found the eye of one Brighton Early, a real Commissar Komarovsky type, arch villain and rival of Zhivago's, Rod Steiger's arresting cinematic presence shining in Brighton's self-important eyes, the sideways glace, locked a little too long on one thing or another, like something in his periphery never seemed quite right.

Brighton was a county health inspector, though none of us knew it when he first came into Trotsky's. He said he was curious about the place, tried The Khrushchev and liked it, then later, aside to Herbie, said:

"Pretty good food, but I never liked that particular commie. A trouble-maker. I knew that chicken-shit would back down in Cuba."

Brighton was in several times, and we should have seen it coming, should have ducked and covered.

"What a wuss," Brighton said of The Gorbachev, as the gravy oozed onto his meat. "Glasnost. Loser."

Afterward, Brighton showed Herbie his county I.D. and wondered how it was he only served Stoli at the bar.

"You got some kind of Rooskie kickback happening here, or what?" he said.

But none of Brighton's Steigerian sideways curiosities compared with when he tried The Putin.

Herbie and I swung our barstools about-face in anticipation of Brighton's digging into The Putin. He sat placidly at his table, hands laid comfortably each side of his hammer-and-sickle placemat atop the red-white-and-blue tablecloth. When the train exited the Trans-Siberian tunnel, The Putin stood especially tall on the flatcar, for Herbie had told Rasputin to "really load that sucker," thinking this may be the pièce de résistance that would forever ingratiate Brighton at Trotsky's.

The engine steamed to a stop, flatcar perfectly aligned with Comrade Brighton's table. He reached and set the platter in front of him, took hold of the massive burger with both hands, and jammed as much as he could into his Steigerian mouth.

He chewed once.

Twice.

His eyebrows arched in a way that could have been culinary consent or condemnation.

He swallowed, then stuck out his tongue. With an index finger, he scraped a layer of black fish eggs off his taste buds and flicked the dark goo onto his plate.

"These fish eggs ain't cooked!" he said, now, uncharacteristically, with one Steigerian eye on Herbie and the other askew, aimed at the locomotive chugging back into the kitchen.

Herbie rushed to Brighton's table.

"They come that way," he said. "Raw."

"I know, but I'm talking about cross-contamination." Brighton rose and headed into the kitchen with Herbie trailing. "I'll bet you got raw commie crap next to corn-fed American ground beef!"

Rasputin, who'd heard everything through the swinging door, said, "Well, I keep them eggs and raw burgers separated like they taught me. Besides, them eggs ain't Volga Beluga. They're American Pride Caviar, only nine bucks an ounce. So them burgers and caviar are American, all the way."

I could tell Rasputin had our Steigerian nemesis temporarily baffled, ideologically idle.

We waited.

Finally, Comrade Brighton shivered back to reality.

"Uh, it's still not right. I mean, what if someone with a fish allergy eats that hamburger thinking it's only a burger. You're gonna kill someone."

I shrugged, looked at Herbie, then Comrade Brighton headed for the pantry, and, after a time, returned swinging the fattest, blackest, deadest rat I'd ever seen by the tail, its mouth smeared with blue mashed potato and jaws clamped tight on one of Khrushchev's sausage missiles.

Well, as if the ravenous rodent wasn't enough, weeks we had more inspections by members of what was called the Central Committee for the Protection of General Health. The Committee discovered Rasputin'd been bluing the potatoes with a cheap carcinogenic food dye from, where else, Red China. And Tuesday Parka Nights? Forget it. There were forms to fill out. Fines to pay. Herbie had to attend what the Committee called mandatory "prophylactic encounters," designed to prevent further infractions.

Herbie temporarily closed the place up when we discovered that Trotsky's may be, in one Committee member's parlance, 'rehabilitated,' a fancy word for asked to make expensive renovations.

People moped around Whitehouse, talking like Trotsky's was closing for good, asking one another, "Why?"

Why? Now they asked why?

I needed the place, that's why, someplace, anyplace, I could go and just be me—or Zhivago, or whomever. Someone, someplace!

Same night Herbie shut the place up, I joined him there. He broke out some Iron Cities, saddled-up next to me at the bar, and we got into those bad boys. I took a long pull on mine and, when Herbie was looking longingly at his mothballed Siberian Railway, secretly gave my barstool a brief, 360-celebratory whirl. At the least, Herbie and I were having a few, just like old times.

I consoled him.

"Just think of this commie stuff as merely a failed experiment. Learn from it. Move on."

Herbie grunted.

"Look, lay low awhile, fix the place up a little, then reopen as the Train Wreck. Heck, you could name it 'Another Train Wreck.' What do you think of that? Give it another go, you know, with good old-fashioned American knowhow."

We were quiet then. I stared into my Iron City, the way you know something that ought to happen may never happen. I was so caught up gazing at the mesmerizing golden meniscus in my mug, I didn't notice Herbie slip out back.

"Oh, Frida!" I heard him lament.

I took my Iron City in my fist and joined him outside.

"Are you okay?" I asked.

Herbie grunted again, then sat down at a picnic table, pointed his telescope at the Moon, and put one eye to the focal tube.

"What're you looking at?"

He was studious in his posture, thumb and forefinger on the focus knob, bringing something into clarity.

"We're right there." Herbie backed away from the telescope and gestured at it. "Take a look."

"I'm not looking at anything," I said, feeling the Iron City, a strange new nastiness growing in my gut.

"It's the Clavius Crater, with five smaller impacts inside, in the shape of a smile. It's the Cheshire's face and grin, same shape as Whitehouse. I promise you."

I reached out and swatted his telescope so it spun two 360s on the tripod.

"I'm not looking at anything," I said, louder.

"Why not?"

That damned question.

"Herbie," I whispered, held my breath and let it go all at once. "Not again."

"But we're up there!" he said.

"No we're not," I said, dreading the arrival of Alice, recently of Wonderland, in Whitehouse.

"I know you believe," he said. "I've been watching you. You can't hide it from me."

I finished the dregs of my Iron City, felt sorry for Herbie. He'd never once played the belief card with me.

So I stuck my inebrious eye to Herbie's telescope and, sure as shit, there on the Moon it looked like the Cheshire grinning at me.

I never admitted it to Herbie.

When I walked home, I was reminded how it was high summer in Whitehouse, cornstalks rustling, crickets bleating, most folks asleep in their homes, stars strewn overhead seeming so close I could reach up and pull one down.

When I got home, I was no longer feeling my Iron City. It was something more. I felt traveled and worldly, wiser for days the Trans-Siberian Railway came to Whitehouse, the way it must feel when you've traveled the whole world and back, and return the hero, happy to be home, happy to find not much has changed, only you secretly hope one little thing might have.

Herbie had me again, that damned old dreamer.

I went into my kitchen, found Pearl at the sink, pressed myself against her backside, whispered, "Lara."

She was looking out the kitchen window, far off, in the direction of a place and time we may have thought we knew once, and may never know again.

"I ain't your Lara no more," she said.

THE BIG HEALY

Out a window of Ford Motor Company Junior High, beyond the crabapple tree and its abandoned nest, I watched three power stacks pour a strange brew of soot and steam upward to mingle with a metal-gray stratum of clouds. Inside our eighth-grade English classroom, lights were off, television set to WKYC Cleveland, educational programming, nattering lines of *The Scarlet Letter*, vexing me with what might have passed for Dimmesdale's "strange disquietude" had it not been for the Healy kid, a lanky, red-headed, cross-eyed boy who'd created a bubble-filled wad of spit hanging precariously from his pursed lips, ready any moment to drip onto the cover of Hawthorne's book, onto the 'A' on Hester Prynne's chest.

Then in walked my father. Everyone knew he was my father. My father who taught Math at Ford Junior High. No one was surprised to see him. But they were surprised when he grabbed the TV dial and clicked a couple numbers to the right, and there it was, only minutes old, President Kennedy's motorcade and the assassination.

The Big Healy slurped the defamatory spit wad back into his mouth.

Miss Surratt sidled up to my father in front of the TV. They stood side-by-side, like a couple at a drive-in movie, two heads silhouetted in the electric glow of the screen. Then their odd moment of romance ended. Forever. My father rocked back on his heels and turned to glance at me. He ran a hand through the blonde bristles of his crew cut and down the back of his neck where skin bulged in two red humps against his stiff white collar. Miss Surratt nuzzled closer to him, as if to insist on that special human warmth people want in moments like the shooting of a beloved president.

"Well," my father sighed. Everyone heard it, that 'well,' his dolorous, deadly 'well,' 'well' that passeth understanding. "Well," he excreted a second time, "it's about time someone shot that commie bastard."

THE BIG HEALY

Miss Surratt turned to my father. Her morning makeup heaved and cracked along fault lines in her forehead, strange hunks of Cover Girl mingling with the creepy gray-blue light. The entire left side of her stealth, girdled body convulsed and coiled outward from my father. She started crying and pounding my father's chest with her fists until she'd pounded him clear through the doorjamb and into the hallway. She back-kick-slammed the steel door shut and started screaming at him in the hallway, words muffled by the door, words I couldn't understand, but sounds that did pass for understanding.

I slid down in my desk as far as I could, without my fanny flat-out hitting the floor. I reached up and ran a thumbnail in the left groove of the letter 'H' carved into my desk by the Big Healy, one letter in one of the more subtle expressions he'd carved into many desktops.

YOU'RE GOING TO HELL

Or some such Healyism.

From his desk across the aisle, the Big Healy stared at me like he had green Coke bottles at the back of his eyes. His expression was strange, not like him, not his usual gloating smile. It was cold, indifferent. His crossed-eyes seemed to wobble, then float in his head, as if they would fall straight out. Then they'd freeze and seem nearly straight, a cold, sober expression, warmer than usual, not the general scorn he showed other kids, but meant for me, only me, and I knew in his icy stare and my cowering glance that we shared a very special knowledge.

Because of what my father'd said, from that moment forward I would be the Most Hated Kid at Ford Motor Company Junior High, not the Big Healy.

The Most Hated Kid was dead.

Long live the Most Hated Kid.

I closed my eyes. I started praying. I didn't know what to say. But I did my best. Kennedy had been shot but wasn't dead yet.

> *Hail Mary,*
> *God please save the President*
> *in the hour of my need . . .*

Then the doctor at Dallas's Parkland Memorial Hospital came up to the microphone and said Kennedy was dead. I kept praying my Hail Mary. I partly opened my eyes. The Big Healy was gaping at me, bottle-eyed. I wanted to say, "Can't you do something about your eyes?" But I knew it assured his retaliation. Kids recalled massive wads of gum in hair, books scattered to the far corners of Ford Junior High's hallways.

Other kids swung around in their seats and glared at me. They expected something. I didn't know what, though with Miss Surratt and my father both in the hallway, I did have one option. I reached back for the only thing I could think of, something I'd perfected in the months before the Kennedy catastrophe, something that had catapulted me to fame among my classmates, the coolest thing I'd ever come up with, but something I rarely used so as not to deflate its value. I reached above my eyes with my fingers. I placed a thumb above each eyelid and tugged on the flesh of the upper regions of my eye sockets. I pulled the skin so tight that the interior, gory red veins stood out. At the same time, I rolled my eyeballs so far down in their sockets all that remained for horrified viewers were two blinding-white eyeballs, glistening and gliding in pools of their own blood and gore. When I allowed my eyes to return to their normal positions in my head, I looked around. Kids still glared at me. Not one utterance of "Gross, Roller!" Not one bone of horror for this dog. And in those moments of their glaring, I accepted my fate, my descent to what had been the Big Healey's Throne of Shame. Not even my patented Roller Eyes could ever change it. That's my story. Maude Roller's story. Maude for Maudlin, Maude for Maugham, Maude for Weeping in Bondage.

When Miss Surratt returned from pounding my father's chest and screaming at him in the hall, her face and hands were purple as crabapples. Her hair was soaked where it met her scalp, so it looked like a wig. Her wild eyes floated in front of the blue-gray glare of the TV, like eyes of the *Fifty-Foot Woman* I'd seen on Ghoulardi. When she shut the TV off, her wild eyes shrunk and vanished with the light of the screen.

"You can all go home," she said.

But I didn't want to. I wanted her to put the TV back on, to see if maybe the assassination had all just been an enactment, a hoax, like *War of the Worlds*, something, anything but what it was.

I waited until all the other kids left, then silently passed by Miss Surratt, who sat at her desk, turned to the window. She wasn't looking at the crabapple tree, its nest, or the Ford Plant. She seemed to be focused on a spot far away, not far away in the sense of distance, but in the sense of time. I couldn't tell if it was sometime in the future or in the past. I tried to follow her stare with my eyes, but got lost, and instead noticed two sky-blue eggshells in the abandoned nest of the crabapple tree. That past spring a red-winged blackbird had bashed in the eggs and sucked them dry.

When I got out in the hallway, the Big Healy strutted up to me. In one fist he held the copy of *The Scarlet Letter* he'd mutilated with a blue Bic pen. No one had ever seen the Big Healy carrying a book, any book, let alone something literary. His gloating seemed to bend him back a little, so his spine was arched like a bow. At that angle, looking down at me, his eyes seemed even more crossed. He was so smug I scarcely noticed his trademark T-shirt with brown bearing grease smudged about his naval area in a circle resembling Stonehenge, or the holes in the knees of his jeans textured with tiny white threads running horizontally like fine Venetian blinds. He was no longer the scum of Ford Motor Company Junior High. He was the Big Healy, a rare bird, a real icon of verbal culture. He read books. But I shouldn't have blamed the Big Healy by himself. Even Hawthorne's book, its cheap paper backing, its cracked-glue spine poking pathetically out the Big Healy's fist, seemed to gloat and condemn me.

"What were you praying for, Roller?" he said and smacked me in the shoulder with his *Scarlet Letter*. "You hypocrite. You hated the President."

A couple days later, Mr. Payne, the Assistant Principal, came on the PA system, "Consistent with the nation's mourning our great loss." School was cancelled. I headed home for two "death days," with, so far as I knew, the only man in America, besides Oswald, who hated Kennedy enough to want him dead. My father. I dreaded it. As I walked home along Holland Road, I realized I hadn't communicated with my father in a long time, other than in grunts and waves. I knew all along he'd hated Kennedy, heard his diatribes about "Another one of them long-hair liberals who wants to be Pope of America," the sort of utterances I thought came more of his heartburn after his weekly dinner of fried chicken stomachs than of gutsy political convictions. But I never thought it would affect me. Maude. Former coolest kid with the amazing Roller Eyes. Maude, at the zenith of her popularity, one who had distilled from the chaotic and confusing assortment of infinite things a kid could do, one talent, one look, one defining, hilarious countenance. Maude. Anchored by her craft's honestly, simplicity, and originality.

But now?

God. I was ruined.

When I arrived home, I passed my mother in the kitchen washing apples in the sink and went straight to my bedroom. That evening, when I heard my father going through the house and into his bedroom, I went straight in, first time I'd ever done such a bold thing, and found him as I knew I would, lying in bed, his legs crossed, the spit-shine of his old Navy-issue shoes gleaming under the globe light, dead center of the spackled ceiling. His eyes were dead forward into the pages of *Time*.

"Father," I said, "forget about the President. You may as well have assassinated *me*!"

Nothing in his bedroom moved. Not one spit-shined toe, not one particle of light in reflection, not one follicle of his hair, not one speck of dandruff. Even house dust, some of which I was sure would gossip at my bodacious outburst, lay silent on sills, the dresser, everywhere. I stood there waiting for his response. Stood there realizing for the first time that some processes in the Universe were dreadfully silent, irreversible, as though I was marooned on a pink-blue coral shoal of the Bikini Islands after an H-Bomb test, white ashen flakes falling all around me, through silence, like a first snow, then never snowing again, poisoning everything forever. My father's dolorous, explosive words in Miss Surratt's class had not only ruined my life. In their wake was only silence and grief. He had cut me adrift into the cruel and uncaring student body of Ford Motor Company Junior High. I waited. He didn't say anything. No reply. Nothing. And so, in return, I left him there, alone, with *Time*, forever.

In the kitchen, my mother was more communicative, but no help in the matter of my public disgrace. She presided over a little pile of long, helical apple peels on the Formica counter. I took one peel and began to rake it over my bottom teeth to scrape off its remaining flesh.

"Now the whole world knows Father wanted Kennedy dead," I said. "Jesus, the FBI will open a file on us."

She took the peel from me and set it with other scraps in the little pile.

"Dear," she said, "your father has strong convictions." Then she added, "Dear, your father is also insecure."

I'd heard these before. These two excuses for my father were manifold and covered nearly everything my father said and did, including his reaction to Presidential assassinations.

But if coming home was one crisis, then going back to school was another. The whole Kennedy thing was serious, not like refusing to let the Big Healy cheat off my *Scarlet Letter* examination. Kids had understood that, even admired me for it, seeing as the Big Healy had been the former most hated and feared kid in school. But my being Most Hated Kid was different. Mere Maude, Mousy Maude. I would only be hated, not feared. Getting all the ridicule from them and giving back none of the dread. It wasn't fair. What's more, the second day I was home, Jack Ruby killed Oswald and that night I dreamed Ruby busted out of jail and came after my father—and me. The morning I was to return to school I lay in bed and held my breath to make my face turn into blotches of white, red, and blue. With my respiratory system thusly bottled, my mom walked in and saw me in my strange chromatic state.

"Sick?" she said. "We'll have your father come up."

It was no use. I vigorously shook my head.

I prayed with blue lips:

> *Hail Mary,*
> *God please burn down Ford Motor Company Junior High*
> *in the hour of my need . . .*

I dressed and went downstairs to find her ironing. I made my patented Roller Eyes at her, peeled my eyelids up with my fingertips, held them that way a full five seconds. She stopped her iron mid-glide over one of my father's shirts. She cocked it back to rest on the board. The iron sighed a little, followed by a puff of steam.

"You know," she said, "if you go making eyes like that all the time, your face is going to stay that way." I let my upper eyelids pop down into place with two wet ticking sounds. "That's better," she went on, "you don't want to be permanently ugly the rest of your life, do you? All goofy looking?"

I stared at my mom. She was in her magenta terrycloth housecoat and matching slippers, her pink-tinted blond hair piled high on her head, miles into the stratosphere, so high that wisps of errant and fatigued locks encircled it like pink stratus clouds about a mountain peak I'd seen on the cover of *Heidi*, or was it *Heidi's Mountain*? Something like it. I'd have given anything to *be* Heidi, to grab hold and forever hang onto her grandfather's beard-locks with my precious little fists. Then I was sure I could bear my return to Ford Motor Company Junior High. I could bear any future of ignominy, back full of spit-wads and kick-me notes. If only I had those reassuring long white locks to tug on tight.

My way back to school, I kept watch in the north for some change in the Ford Plant. I prayed for picket signs along the high barbed-wire fence. A strike, closure of the plant, paralyzing the whole community, perhaps even closing my school, its namesake. But there were no signs, nothing. Steam and soot streamed steadily out the stacks, billowed upward, and swelled against a layer of stagnant air, until the whole great ball of dirty vapor broke upward, crested, and carried east, like herds of muscled, gray horses. Would that I had one of them to ride out, away! I followed the galloping shapes of steam as they passed over the Northwestern Railroad tracks and the dump, where I could just make out the high chain-link fence behind which the Healy Brothers lived with their dad who ran the junkyard.

When I got back to school, no one seemed to notice me. The first half-day I may as well have been the ghost of Kennedy, watching their sad expressions, with all my ghostly urges to come straight up to them, invisible, and whisper in their ears, "It's okay. It's not so bad. So I'm dead. Assassinated. I don't blame you. Life goes on."

Or would Kennedy's ghost have said that?

That afternoon, Miss Surratt stood stiff as a ladder in front of our class; from her top rung, two long waves of hair ran down the sides of her head like waterslides, lacquered with hair spray that had to be a government secret. She was parked into a skirt so tight she must've been breathing through her ears. But there were subtle signs of movement. She began wriggling at the hips to assure herself that her spine was straight. And the curl on the right side of her head was sprung. Then she started scratching the inside of one calf with the high heel of her shoe. Finally, she announced we would not be seeing television in her class ever again. The "box," as she now called it, would be removed.

"It's a shock," she went on, suddenly crabapple-faced all over again. "Mr. Kennedy's murder." Her eyes were hollow and faintly glowing, possumish, like she'd become nocturnal. "Sometimes things happen that can't be explained. If any of you would like to talk."

Maybe another kid would have been scared to talk. But after my failed encounter with my father, what had I to lose? When Miss Surratt saw me raise my arm, her eyes seemed to float away from their sockets. She looked all over the room for someone else's arm. Then her eyes floated back, into her head, and rested on me.

"Yes, Maude," she said.

"I'm having trouble sleeping," I said.

"You should!" shouted the Big Healy.

"Quiet, Andrew," Miss Surratt said, sweetly.

"Andrew?" some kid yukked on the other side of the room.

"Quiet!" Miss Surratt said. "Well, dear, Maude," she went on, "when I have trouble sleeping, I just close my eyes and think about my toes and make them vanish. Then I move on to my feet and ankles. I make them vanish. Then my legs. And so on. By the time I'm thinking about my head and making it vanish, I'm already asleep."

I thought: why would I want to make my body vanish? I'd already spent the whole day being Kennedy's ghost and probably would be the rest of my life.

"Miss Surratt," I said, "what if by the time you think about making your head vanish you're not asleep? Should you just go ahead and make it vanish anyway?"

"Stay after class, Maude," she replied. "I want to talk to you."

Then Miss Surratt told us she wanted us to make scrapbooks, anything about Kennedy, his life, his death, anything about Kennedys or Kennedyness. At the time, I would have thought more about the difficulties of completing such a task, but I was too worried about what she wanted with me after class. When the moment arrived and I got up to her desk, I saw she had a copy of *The Feminine Mystique* sitting next to her forest-green grade book.

"What's the Feminine Mystique?" I asked, hoping to distract her from whatever it was she wanted me for.

She looked at me a long time, the way you look at someone when you can't decide whether to invite them to your house or not.

"It's the opposite of the Male Mystique," she replied and plopped her green grade book on top of *The Feminine Mystique* so only the letters '*que*' showed. "Never mind that," she said sweetly. "Maude, I think you know what your father said the other day in class about Mr. Kennedy was terrible. I mean, you *know* it was terrible, right?"

"Yes," I said, "it was definitely terrible."

"Good," she said. "I just want you to know I don't hold you responsible for *him*."

"I know," I said, but had no idea how I was going to complete the Kennedy scrapbook with my father around the house.

Winter had come on. Clouds stretched across the sky like blue-tinged gauze. Plumes from the power stacks no longer rolled under the clouds, but fed straight into their underbellies like umbilical cords, translucent, purple, undulant. It was in such a state of strange incubation that I hatched my plan, a way I could redeem myself at school. Maybe if, against all odds, I completed the most affectionate, devout, comprehensive, and beautiful Kennedy scrapbook ever, Miss Surratt would ask me to stand with her on the very spot my father had cursed me. Maybe she would publicly acclaim my affection for our dead president. So I set about my task with high seriousness, a seriousness far beyond my years. One night, while upstairs my father and mother reveled in *Make Room for Daddy* followed by *Gunsmoke*, I stole into the crawlspace of our basement, a low, cavernous room, above which gray crossbeams ran, festooned with cobwebs. In a dismal crouch, assisted only by the light of a bare bulb with a rusty chain switch, I cut and juxtaposed black and white images of life—Jackie Kennedy holding her child—and death—Jackie bent sideways in the open limousine with her hands on her husband's chest, mouth open in horror. After a time, I found myself more focused on Jackie than on Jack, a thematic thread I wove through the scrapbook. After that first night, each time I entered the crawlspace to work, I felt a strange love, the kind of love that drew its strength from daily news, things earthly, beautiful and awful, things that, through some mysterious process, found themselves backlit in terrible and essential ways in my mind: the way I set Jackie's dark, mourning shoulder against Jack's bright smile, the way the lace of her wedding dress countered the last oval-shaped ouch of Oswald.

I was overwhelmed by this love, and with hope that I could redeem myself.

> *Hail Mary,*
> *God please let my scrapbook get an A*
> *in the hour of my need . . .*

But was it enough to pray? How could I know? So I continued my creation. I braided red, white, and blue yarn together and threaded it through the eyelets in the pages to bind them, then placed the whole scrapbook in a shiny white plastic folder. On the folder I taped a picture of the eternal flame lit when they buried the President. That was all, that eternal flame, without reference to anything else. I wanted something minimal, tasteful, nothing too terrifying, something that merely hinted at the rich and tragic depths beneath the surfaces of things.

I wanted my A.

Then I ran into a problem, not with the scrapbook itself, but with its byproducts. I had to find a way of disposing of the cut-up newspapers. If my father found them he'd surely be able to match the text with the vacancies in the print and see that someone—me—had an interest in Kennedy or at least Kennedyness, and my mother (on his orders) would call on me to explain myself. I thought about shredding, burning, burying the newspapers, but the fundamental problem was one of material balance. My mother kept a meticulous inventory of my father's newspapers, which were bound with brown twine and stored in the crawlspace until musty and yellow. Sometimes, he'd asked to see a back-issue, some old op-ed on which he'd want to state his convictions or insecurities to Mom. I couldn't dispose of the cutout papers at home, yet I had to make my mom, a sure double-agent of my father's, aware of why the papers had disappeared in the first place.

Back in my bedroom, I agonized over the matter for hours, knowing that as more time passed, it became more likely my mom would discover the missing papers. I stood on my bed and paced awhile, then paused at the window, watching the three plumes from the Ford Plant combine to form a single cloud shaped like a mushroom—no, a hat. In the eventide light, the hat changed from white to blue, and finally to red. Then it came to me, in a vision. I returned to the crawlspace, quickly gathered up all the pages with the Kennedy cutouts and, using knowledge I'd acquired in art class the previous year, fashioned a papier-mâché version of U.S. Sam, letting the papers dry, painting him entirely white, then covering that with red and blue for his top hat and trousers. I used a black magic marker to fashion his face, beard, nose, lips, eyes, and boots. For a finishing touch, I went into my purse, took out the brand new makeup kit I'd acquired after a solid year of bickering with my mother, opened it, broke the mirror off the hinge, and mounted it in U.S. Sam's arms above a tiny banner I'd fashioned.

I WANT YOU!

I let U.S. Sam dry overnight, and the next morning before school found my mom in her kitchen making, what else, an apple pie. I was in luck. She was distracted by some personal tragedy.

"Maude," she sighed and nodded affectionately at her patented double-crusted, rim-reinforced, industrial-strength pie sitting on her stovetop. "That is the last apple pie I will ever make in that oven." I could feel the breath go out of her. "Your father," (who else's father would he be?), "says we have to junk it."

I couldn't believe my good luck. She was nearly comatose with worry over the fate of her stove. I leaned a little toward her, thought about slipping U.S. Sam's compact mirror under her nostrils to see if they were still blowing.

I handed U.S. Sam to her.

"I made this," I squeaked, "with some of Dad's old newspapers."

She listlessly set her apple corer on the counter, took U.S. Sam in one hand, set him on the table, and placed her palm on top of his hat. She turned U.S. Sam around a couple times.

"Didn't you do papier-mâché last year?" she said with a far off voice.

"Yes," I replied, "but this is advanced papier-mâché. It's for Father, a shaving mirror."

"Oh." Her eyes glazed over with vague rainbows like those you get when you heat metal glowing red and then dowse in cold water. She took U.S. Sam by the neck and glided aimlessly into the bedroom where my father again lay thumbing through *Time*.

The night before my Kennedy scrapbook was due, I was so desperate to sleep that I tried Miss Surratt's vanishing body trick. I closed my eyes and focused on my toes. I commanded them to vanish, but they were still there, wriggling as if in joyous laughter, a little chorus of five on each foot, my pinkies contraltos, my big toes baritones. Then I thought I might have been too ambitious to try to get all ten toes to vanish at once. I tried for one nail on my left pinkie toe, but it was no use. It may as well have been the Toenail of Gibraltar. I became depressed with the possibility that not only was I the progeny of a Kennedy-hater, but that a massive failure of the imagination must accompany such a disgraceful inheritance.

Eventually, I got to sleep and had a dream that I'd innovated my patented Roller Eyes so that I could remove my eyeballs from my head altogether, set them places, and walk around blind with blood-sockets, impressing kids to the absolute limits of their wits. One day I'd pop my eyeballs out and the next pop them back in and look perfectly normal. In my dream, it was a fabulous trick, enormously popular with my classmates, until one time I set my eyeballs in the bird's nest in the crabapple tree outside our English window. A red-winged blackbird dove straight out of the gray clouds above the Ford Plant and stole them. I was totally blind.

At first, my blindness was an advantage. Despite all my stumbling around and panic, I was no longer the Most Hated Kid at school but the Most Pitied Kid, replacing Wendy Wetli, who was partially deaf and talked so loud that Miss Surratt cast her to deliver the opening speech of *Henry the Fifth*, in which we were all supposed to imagine horses and sweeping fields of battle, all crammed onto a tiny stage. Such was the nightmare that had begun with my father's dolorous words, all of history clawing its way up my back like a frightened alley cat, then using my back as its stage—and digging in. But in my dream, indulgence in self-pity soon gave way to sheer panic that my eyes had been stolen! Day after day I clumsily climbed the crabapple tree, feeling inside the nest with my hand to detect if the blackbird had returned my eyes.

When I consulted Miss Surratt about what to do, she said, "Go, Child, into the Wilderness, and live among the Heathen. Find an animal's eyeballs that will fit your eye sockets. Convince it to give you its eyes."

I did just as Miss Surratt instructed. I crossed the railroad tracks, past the dump and the Healys' junkyard, into the Wilderness. I wandered there for years (or so it seemed in my dream) because the only animals I could find were timid robins hopping about with tiny eyeballs and mountain-shouldered work horses clopping around with enormous eyeballs. Such a strange wilderness. And neither type of eyeball fit my eye sockets, but I needed something to see with, so, eventually, I came upon a robin tugging at a hapless worm. It opened its beak and the worm sprung back into the earth.

"My eyes are tiny," the robin said. "Everything you see will be much too small."

But I begged the robin, which eventually felt sorry for me. The robin clawed out an eye, handed it to me, but kept one eye to see with.

Days after that, I ran across a work horse grazing in a clearing.

"I'm desperate," I sobbed to the horse and cajoled him a long while.

"Alright," the massive beast sighed. "You may take one eye." Its enormous shoulders slumped a bit. "But everything you see with it will be much too big."

I put the horse's eyeball into my eye socket next to the robin's eyeball. I found that seeing too big and too small at the same time made me terribly dizzy. Nevertheless, I returned to civilization, that is, Ford Motor Company Junior High.

I immediately reported to Miss Surratt with my new eyeballs. I said, "I've done as you asked." I cocked my head back a little to keep my tiny robin eyeball from rolling out. "This is the best I can do."

"Well," she replied, inspecting my new eyes, "then you have learned, Young One."

"Learned what?

"Not to be goofing around," she laughed. "You look ridiculous!"

The dream of my eyes made me wonder if I should ever follow Miss Surratt's instructions. Maybe my completing the scrapbook for her was pointless. When I woke, beams of a red, round early-December sun crawled out the cylindrical edges of the steel stacks of the Ford Plant. My eyes burned and felt gritty. I felt for them. I was so relieved my eyes were intact, I sat up and, with new hope, reached under my bed, took up my Kennedy scrapbook, and set it on my lap. It was as beautiful as I remembered in those secret, euphoric moments of creation in the crawlspace. I ran my hands over the cold plastic cover, and continued to rub, hoping I could warm it up. Then I feared that plastic was too cold a material for the cover, not elegiac enough. I thought about using cardboard, cheaper and warmer. But time was short, so I stuffed the scrapbook in my book bag and got myself off to school.

When I got situated at my desk in English, like an idiot I forgot to keep my scrapbook under covers until Miss Surratt collected it. The Big Healy leaned out into the aisle and peeked at it. His crossed eyes gleamed with excitement when he saw my white plastic cover, my red, white, and blue braided bindings. He doubled over with silent laughter.

I instinctively shot him my patented Roller Eyes.

"Maude," Miss Surratt said sweetly. "Come up here." As I traveled through the thick silence of my classmates to the front of the classroom, she added, "Show me what you just did."

"What I just did?"

"You know what you did," she said.

Being on the bottom rung of believability, I had nothing to lose by showing her the truth. I made my Roller Eyes at Miss Surratt. The Big Healy nearly fell out of his desk. I let my eyelids pop back into place, tick, tick.

"Now," Miss Surratt said, "I want you to keep your eyes like that until I say you can quit."

So I did, while other kids in the class went from murmuring hysterics to dead silence. Time passed and my eyeballs started to dry out. My brain began to race, wondering why Miss Surratt's punishments always amounted to the same thing. You were made to keep on doing the stupid thing you had been doing, like when she made the Big Healy spit one hundred times into the wastebasket until his saliva glands could barely function. Or when she made him stay bent over like a carnival contortionist, his head nearly on the floor, staring sideways and toward the ceiling.

"Andrew," she asked the Big Healy that time, "tell me why you were in such a strange position."

"Search me," he replied.

But everyone knew he'd been looking up Miss Surratt's skirt as she walked by his desk.

If single acts of stupidity were the essence of comedy, then infinitely repeated ones added up to tragedy. It was terrible justice. And so far as I knew no one in the history of Ford Motor Company Junior High had ever had to repeat the stupid thing they'd done as long as I did. My Roller Eyes were drying, shriveling. They felt salty, like roasted nuts.

Finally, I panicked.

"Miss Surratt!"

"Alright!" she said.

After that, I knew Miss Surratt hated me, knew it completely. We hadn't even the Feminine Mystique in common, whatever it was. The only question was whether such a hate as hers could be reversed by the graceful and redemptive qualities of a true work of art, my Kennedy scrapbook. As I settled into my desk, rubbing my eyes, temporarily but legally blind, I felt for the cover of my scrapbook. It was there, cold, smooth, reassuring, with all the astonishment and pain and horror—and my hopes—pressed inside. All during my ordeal I'd been terrified the Big Healy might steal my scrapbook. But it was safe from him. I passed my Kennedy scrapbook to the kid ahead of me, and then watched it bound, hand to hand, up the row to the front, where Miss Surratt clutched it, along with all the others, to her chest. Then it disappeared into a drawer of her desk.

We never knew when we were getting papers back from Miss Surratt. One day we'd come in and all she did was pass them back, pages fluttering and kids stuffing them in their bags, some groaning in near despair because we were required to have our parents sign them and bring them back. This might have put another major obstacle in my path to redemption when I realized that no matter what grade she gave me I'd have to take the Kennedy scrapbook home to my parents. But I decided to forge my mom's signature and, considering the nature of my dilemma, it was worth the risk.

A week later, my scrapbook came back to me. I tried hard to conceal my grade from the Big Healy, but, as always, he had the height advantage, and besides, I had paused a little too long to read Miss Surratt's note inside the cover of my scrapbook:

I KNOW YOU DIDN'T HAVE ANY HELP FROM HOME.
A.

The Big Healy leaned in and looked at my A. He stretched back in his seat and smiled, not a mean smile, but a giddy sort of smirk, tinged with a look of confidence in my hypocrisy. I'd gotten my A, but sensed that the Big Healy was readying himself to announce my A to the whole class. I had to think fast. Isn't this what I'd wanted? Not quite! Not the Big Healy sarcastically revealing my A to the world. Oh! I glanced out the window at the abandoned robin's nest, its eggs eviscerated by the red-winged blackbird. And that moment, more than anything, I wanted blackbird eyes. I wanted red-winged blackbirdness. I wanted to dive out of the sky and pluck out what I wanted, what I needed, to put my beak into my silent father's brain and twist his gray matter about until he screamed. What on earth had my father been thinking, standing there, bathed in cathode rays, telling the world he hated Kennedy, wanted him dead. Had those cathode rays affected his mind? I wished my father had been handy, but all I had was the Big Healy. I lurched upward, out of my seat. I was going for the Big Healy's red, freckled neck with my hands, but before I could leave my desk, the Big Healy suddenly slid into the aisle and fell to his knees beside me, clutching his disfigured copy of *The Scarlet Letter* to his chest, turning blue, groaning, spittle rippling out between his lips in a thin foam.

I flopped back into my seat in amazement.

"Maude," Miss Surratt said, clopping down the aisle toward us. Her big waterslide curls vibrated like diving boards just after someone had jumped off. "What is the problem?"

I said, "I don't know," feeling that tickle in the stomach when you know you haven't done something but may somehow be at fault.

Miss Surratt galloped back to the front of the class.

She jacked up on the tiny toe areas of her high heels, and then pressed the intercom button.

"Mr. Payne," she said. "I need you!"

Then she trotted back and stood staring over the Big Healy, who was by then on his side, rolled up like a boiled shrimp, jaws shut tighter than a clam's, groaning like he was underwater, the way I'd imagined the crew of the *U.S.S. Thresher* submarine had groaned, lost forever, eight thousand feet down.

Mr. Payne rushed into the room with a glum look on his face.

"Maude Roller," he said. "What is going on?"

I stood. I guess I'd intended on standing, ready to be judged. They looked at me. Miss Surratt, Mr. Payne, all the kids in my class. They looked at the Big Healy writhing at my feet. Mr. Payne shouted again.

"What have you done to him?"

Everyone stared at me, except the Big Healy, who now gaped vacantly at the ceiling. 'THE SCAR' in Hester's tale showed through his blue finger-grip. I saw everything in my classmates' and teachers' eyes, Oswald's death-ouch, riderless horses, LBJ's tight-set pulsating jaw, Jackie, O Jackie! O grief! I saw everything in black and white that couldn't be explained.

"How," I said.

I reached for my eyes with my fingers.

"The fuck."

I rolled them downward in their sockets.

"Should I know!"

THE BIG HEALY

And everything went white on my side of things.

Soon, the Big Healy came out of his epileptic fit and explained what had happened to him. Mr. Payne took him out of the room to see the school nurse. Then Mr. Payne came back and suspended me from Ford Motor Company Junior High. Me. Maude Roller. Not for attempting to throttle the Big Healy, sure suicide, but for foul utterances that shocked the sensibilities of Mr. Payne and Miss Surratt, perhaps even more than my father's words about our dead president.

I suppose some kids go straight home to their parents when they are suspended from school. They accept the punishment given them. But how could I? With my Kennedy scrapbook under my arm? With what Miss Surratt had written in my Book of the Dead, my Hieroglyphics of Hope?

When I got outside the school, the air felt fine for a December day. The cloud ceiling was high over the Ford Plant, a kind of gray turquoise. Plumes of bone-colored smoke rose thickly, drifted over the city, dissipated, and vanished. When the cloud ceiling was high like that, the plant seemed a long way off, the edge of the world farther than I ever remembered it. But then the sun came out under the cloud ceiling, lit up the stacks, and changed their plumes to blue-orange, and the horizon behind the freight yards seemed closer. It was then I turned from my usual way home, off Holland Road, and followed Engle Road to the Northwestern Railroad tracks.

I crab-crawled up one side of an embankment made of gravel stones, big as fists, tinged with creosote, the smell so strong the bridge of my nose tingled, tightened, and fell numb. I crossed the tracks and slid down the other side of the embankment. A short distance into a grove of poplar saplings, I reached the outskirts of the Dump, where great dunes of waste sand and ash from the plant rolled out before me. I jutted into the dunes with the toes of my Hush Puppies, sending little puffs about my ankles. In some areas the dunes were so old they preexisted the poplar saplings sprouting out of them, some with bare-knuckled roots showing, clutching at the sand the way I'd once imagined Heidi had hold of her grandfather's beard-locks.

Soon, I reached a land of a thousand tin cans lying scattered about, half-sunken into the dunes. Farther east, I found a little metropolis, half-risen from the gray sands, clumps of cast-off stoves, fridges, and TVs, papers fluttering among them like little flags. There, I came upon my mother's discarded stove. I stood a few paces from it, not believing my eyes, the way you can't believe something when you see it removed from where it has been a long, long time. I'd intended to bury my Kennedy scrapbook in the wasteland. Instead, I hopped on my mother's old stove, sat, and watched the plant's plumes coil up underneath the high cloud ceiling until they rolled into one vaporous iris, dilated against the fading blue-orange light. The iris stared at me. I gave back as good as I got from that vaporous eye, until I couldn't look at it anymore.

Then I spotted him, there in the sand, my U.S. Sam, his papier-mâché top hat and one ear sticking out a black plastic garbage bag. I hopped down, knelt, and took him onto the stovetop with my scrapbook. I turned him around and looked at my face in my broken-off makeup mirror glued into his arms. I searched my face in my U.S. Sam makeup kit mirror. I gauged the gaps between my eye sockets and eyeballs to see if they had widened at all, looked for any sign of permanent distortion resulting from my patented Roller Eyes. I couldn't spot any change, but then thought, seeing that the growing dusk had gone from blue-orange to deep green, you can't know the long-term effects of things you do to yourself every day.

I closed my eyes. If I was destined to be goggle-eyed, alone, and ugly, I didn't want to be visible anymore. I tried once more to make my toes vanish but couldn't. I tried to start with my head, thinking that if I could get my head to vanish the rest would follow. For a moment, I thought I had succeeded. The tender part of one arm touching the plastic cover of my Kennedy scrapbook seemed to numb. Then the tips of my fingers about U.S. Sam's neck began to tingle into insensibility. By starting with making my head vanish, I thought I might have innovated Miss Surratt's vanishing body trick. But then I wondered: how could my head have vanished since I needed my head to know my body parts were vanishing?

I decided that if the vanishing trick didn't work, I'd hop off my mother's stove and bury myself in the sand like remains of a mummy, Maude, the macabre monk who died with barbarians at the gate, twilight of a civilization, clutching the essentials of her era, in one hand U.S. Sam and in the other her Kennedy scrapbook, her preserved physiognomy a medical enigma, distended shapes of her eye sockets a fit subject for future scientists.

When I opened my eyes, I stared not into the timeless ignominious future of an ancient relic, but at the junkyard, where the Big Healy sat on the black, bashed-in hood of some cobbled Nova. He grinned his Healy grin, county-to-county, his mangled copy of *The Scarlet Letter* resting on one thigh, relishing my suspension. The middle finger of his right hand shot up.

I shouted at him.

"Bastard!"

He shook his cross-eyed head like he couldn't hear me and continued grinning, wagging his accusatory middle finger. And then I knew I would have to chance it. Behind me were the precarious fortunes of enlightenment, Ford Motor Company Junior High, Father's murderous convictions and insecurities, Mother's almighty pies, Miss Surratt's mystique. But ahead of me?

I took up my U.S. Sam, my Kennedy scrapbook. I closed my eyes. I closed them tight, then hopped down from my mother's stovetop and headed Healy's way. When I reached the galvanized link fence, Healy slid his worthless ass off the hood of the Nova and slithered over to the fence. I tossed my scrapbook and U.S. Sam over the top links. He caught them and set them on the hood. When I hopped the fence, he was still grinning, standing by the caved-in bumper, waving his *Scarlet Letter* over his head like some crazy kind of Keats having just cracked Chapman's *Homer*. When he started picking his nose, I dashed over to the hood and retrieved my scrapbook and U. S. Sam.

"Hey, Roller," he said, leaned back against the gnarled grill, and tapped the spine of the Hawthorne's book against the hole where a headlight had been. "I finished it."

"What do you want?" I spat. "A medal?"

I faced him squarely. Maude for Maugre. Maude in spite of Maude.

He gaped at my U.S. Sam and scrapbook, then grinned, so I told him if he ever said anything to anyone about me coming to the junkyard, or about the 'A' on my scrapbook, I'd get my father's .38 and gut-shoot him like Ruby gut-shot Oswald. I'd gut-shoot him so he'd not only *be* cross-eyed, but *feel* cross-eyed in the extreme. Then I set my scrapbook and U.S. Sam back, stuck my thumbs to my eyelids, made my Roller eyes at him, and, while everything went blazing red and white, while I thought I had him in my appalling patented blind gaze, he tried to kiss me!

I hit him upside the head. I prayed.

> *Hail Mary,*
> *God please let the Big Healy*
> *try and kiss me just one more time.*
> *I'll bite his tongue off and spit it back at him*
> *in the hour of my need . . .*

"Alright, Jesus, Maude," he said, digging in his nose again. "I'll tell them you didn't hate the President."

And so many years I believed him. I really did. I even thought the Big Healy might put everything back to normal. But I've come to know that whatever the Big Healy told them has never made a difference. How could it? Forever, Most Hated Kid at Ford Motor Company Junior High. Forever, Kennedy's assassin. You've seen me. I know you have. I fly, age after age, upon my galloping gray horses, among blue-tinged November clouds, blinded white, in my robin's half-shell saddle, high in east winds, cracked, dry. I fly alone, frozen, in this land of dead presidents. Forever yours, Maude.

COMMIE CHRISTMAS

Bunk aloft, I kicked off my bedspread embroidered with a Redstone rocket racing toward a deep blue quadrant of space. I swung past the safety rail and gazed down, through clearing mists of sleep, to see Allen's bunk, bunker really, where he cowered from unseen foes, in fetal coil, thumb in mouth, unnatural at the age of six.

"Get your thumb out your mouth," I said, feeling like that thumb, Christmas vacation, 1962, sucked into a shriveled existence as his older brother, bunkmate, sharing everything.

Allen's thumb popped out, revealed buck teeth, the result of constant vectors of thumb-force tugging outward. His eyes swam and opened, unperturbed by Mom's slamming the dryer door and Dad's hammering in the half-basement before going to work, his project to relocate me to that darker region of the house, where the furnace growled hourly into flame and breathed life into our Cleveland split-level.

"What do Santie's reindeer eat, anyway?" Allen asked.

Santie was the diminutive term Dad had used growing up, though he stopped using it after he got his job at NASA's Lewis Research Center, some top secret project. But Allen picked up the word. Only weeks after the Cuban Missile Crisis ended, Allen went on and on about Santie, as if the world had never been on the brink of annihilation. I wouldn't have known about the Missile Crisis, only Dad had set up the old Westinghouse in the half-basement and I snuck down to watch coverage of the blockade. The TV sputtered—

> *mostly sunny and cold*
> *Cuban missile crisis expected to have little*
> *effect on the cost of living*
> *talks take on a graver aspect*
> *full retaliatory response possible*
> *flurries ending later this evening*

"Reindeer eat atomic apples," I informed Allen.

"Will we find reindeer shit in the snow?"

"Only if you step in it."

"But what will it look like?"

"Glowing," I said, hooked my toes in the spindles of the footboard of my bunk, swooped in lower, hovered over him. "Just shut up about reindeers. Santie's a commie, anyway."

"Is not!" His words shot straight past a suspicious fragment of dried oatmeal cloying in a corner of his mouth. I doubted Allen even knew what a commie was, only that it had to be bad, but I didn't care. I made such ugly accusations—even about someone like Santie—and a part of me knew they weren't true. But then I wondered: If I could think Santie was a commie, then it could be true; otherwise I wouldn't have thought it in the first place. And if Santie was a commie, then it explained why he never brought me the one thing I wanted above all, the one luxurious thing no self-respecting commie would ever ask for, a Nine Transistor Realtone Radio, because if he got it he'd be sent to a gulag. No other kid I knew had a transistor radio, let alone a Nine Transistor. Santie had failed me, cataclysmically. But the A-bomb, the Missile Crisis, now there was hope! I imagined Dad and Mom embracing, relieved we'd not be nuked into nonexistence, clutching one another, teary eyed, Dad saying, "Maybe, just this once, we ought to get Bud that Nine Transistor Realtone he's been wanting," and Mom blubbering, "Get him anything he wants, anything, no matter how expensive—in case we're blown to bits!"

Allen's translucent thumb rocketed into his mouth, then popped right out.

"If Santie's a commie," he said, "then how come he brings toys to kids?"

"That's exactly why he is a commie. Santie wants to take all the toys and spread them around to everyone, same as what commies want to do with everyone's money."

"So what's wrong with that?"

I rolled a little over the sideboard so I could make eye contact with him. I wanted him to remember this, big brother to little brother, my eyes dead on his, locked tight like the latest missile guidance system I imagined Dad worked on at NASA.

"You know those redheaded, cross-eyed Healy brothers that live next to Regina Mountcastle's? You remember how they chased me down with their big red Schwinns last summer? How they ran me and my new bike clean into the ditch? How I told Dad I'd done it myself because if I said

Healy brothers did it he'd ask me to go after them?

A sucking sound, and the thumb went in. I could hear him working the big digit against his front teeth.

"Do you really think Healy brothers deserve the same as you and me for Christmas? Do you think they deserve the same money and stuff as us? Not everyone deserves the same as everyone else. Especially Healy brothers."

Since we were on the subject of sharing, I leapt down to Allen's bunk and snatched the steel Tonka truck out his bed things. That Tonka had been mine before Dad gave it to Allen, saying, "Share and share alike, Bud." I shot up, regained my bunk, but not before he took hold of the Tonka. I clamped my toes onto the spindles of the footboard.

"Gimme that truck, you little commie," I said.

I hauled up on the Tonka, he hauled down, until I had him moving back and forth, let him think we were in a stalemate of awesome forces—then I let go.

After I conked Allen with the Tonka, Mom confined me to our room while Allen paraded about the house, a flesh-colored Band-Aid affixed to his upper lip like a comical dictator's moustache. But I knew Mom would let me out soon. She couldn't resist the Snow Road Cinema, and it wasn't long before she backed the Fairlane out the garage, ordered us into the car, stuck her Yellow Pages to the driver's seat, boosted herself on it, and took off for the Snow Road. Once inside the dark, projector-lit theater, a thin, wicked little smile jetted across her face. When the feature started, *Invasion of the Body Snatchers*, she whispered, "Do NOT tell your dad," and we wagged our heads emphatically in the affirmative. She knew that Dad, our brilliant scientist, had forbidden any of us to have first contact with invaders in film, television, and any form that such invaders might take. "Those movies aren't true," Dad had warned us. Once, I asked him the truth about outer space, what he worked on at NASA. He wrinkled his brow, took his thick, black, horn-rims off, and licked both lenses. "I can't tell you, boy," he said solemnly, then snuck a handkerchief out his hip pocket and wiped the lenses dry. I wondered if the CIA had programmed his lens-licking response. Say an enemy agent asked him about top secret matters. He'd automatically lick his lenses and that would remind him to clam up. Once, just after the Missile Crisis, I told him I wanted the Nine Transistor for Christmas. "We'll see," he said and licked his lenses, obviously hiding something big.

Soon, Mom, Allen and I found ourselves surrounded by slimy pods developing into copies of real people—then disposing of the originals. It happened while the real people slept. When I glanced over at Allen, he slumped sideways in his seat, thumb planted in the frothy soil of his mouth. I shook him awake.

"Hey," I whispered one of those raspy whispers, so loud you may as well have not whispered. "You wanna become an alien or something?" Of course, I knew Allen wasn't an alien; it just came out my mouth—and because of that it seemed true. The Allen that sat next to me might be a copy of the original kid, perhaps some pact commies had with aliens to duplicate Americans and infiltrate the country, which was why Allen hadn't stopped sucking his thumb when normal kids had.

When we returned from the Snow Road, Mom surprised me by ordering my continued incarceration in our bedroom for lacerating Allen's lip. After serving another half-hour, Allen—Pod Kid—came to visit me. I toed a spindle at the footboard of my bunk until it squeaked a little, a sign Allen usually got, one that meant leave me alone. But he jacked up on tiptoes and poked me in a rib with his wet thumb.

"At least Santie's elves ain't commies," he said.

"They're worst of all!" I said. "They slave for Santie in his toyshop. What if they want to be more than toy makers? You think they have a choice?"

"Mom's putting the new tree up. You coming?"

"Do I have a choice?"

I rolled on my side, squinted at him, thinking if I squinted tightly my eyelashes might polarize light just enough to allow me to see Allen's true commie-alien self, O-mouthed and ready to point and squeal at anyone different from him. Then Mom called us, so I followed Allen into the hallway.

Outside bedrooms on the second level, you could see the entire living and dining rooms at one stretch. I loved to gaze out the vast unclaimed space, exist just a little above everything, have it all to myself—except for Santie, that is. His plastic figure sat on the dining room hutch, Buddha-style, laughing behind a Cossack moustache, conspiratorial wink, and Coca-Cola pressed to his jolly red lips. How could such a strange creature be described as anything but a commie agent? Allen passed Commie Claus several times a day, thoughtlessly squeaking, "Hi, Santie!" And just when I thought Santie was the only other claimant to my space, in a far corner of the living room I spotted our new Gleam-All aluminum Christmas tree, with pom-pom branches and special twist needles. Near the base of the metal tree, the electric color wheel ground away, soaking the tree's reflective branches deep red; then yellow, blazing like a solar flare; then deep blue, like a cold, icy inward glare; and finally green, fresh lawn-cut green, reminding me how much I hated winter.

Mom went to her bedroom to fetch a box of trimmings. Pod-boy fell to his knees, galloped on all fours toward the tree, then stood in a trance before the metallic chameleon, until I worried that the Sputnik tree topper might be sending commie instructions out through the limbs and into his impressionable mind.

I grabbed his shoulders. "Snap out of it," I said and shook him hard. "That tree isn't normal. It's a commie tree."

"It's . . . not." One side of his face glowed blue and he seemed puzzled, as if I'd reached some small cluster of normal brain cells in my so-called brother's head.

After Dad got home from NASA, Mom found me in the half-finished basement, announced, "We're going for ice cream." When I didn't reply, she hesitated, just the way I liked her to. "Stay if you like," she added. "We won't be long." Her eyes darted to the cinderblock wall behind my bed, beyond which the Molloys' driveway and house lay. "Call Molloys if you need anything."

She closed the basement door and I heard a rubbery commotion, the three of them suiting up, and Mom's warnings: Allen this, Allen that, Pod Kid silent as ever, then the moment I longed for—they left and I reached for the paperback on my bed, Dickens's *A Christmas Carol*. Cheap, but I liked how the pebbled faux leather surface felt in my hands, the scent of new ink when I stuck my nose to its inner spine. I belonged there, in my cinderblock quarters, buried in snow, no way out except in pages of a novel, eyes devouring word after word as Ebenezer first hears Marley's ghost wail, his clamorous chains on wooden stairs, ascending, higher, closer, all while my spine numbed against the stone wall. After a time, I heard a second chorus of clanking chains seeming to come from outside our house! I read on—hearing Marley's shackles rattling in and out my head, mixed with moaning snowbound wind. I pressed an ear to a cinderblock. The sound was unmistakable. Horrors! Chains! I threw the book aside, crossed the cold clay tiles to the window, saw white flakes, rankled and riotous, careen into uneven walls and soft mounds of snow-covered building materials for new houses under construction. Most houses were dark inside, un-sided, open to elements. Streetlamp light glinted off aluminum backing and insulation. But I found no real source of Marley's lamentation. Was this to be my fate in the wake of the Missile Crisis? Hallucination? Madness? I heard our back door open, Dad's Corvair puttering, Allen stomp upstairs, run water in the sink. Then I heard Dad and Mom come in.

"Snow's getting deep out there," Dad told Mom. "I saw Molloy next door putting chains on his tires. Guess I better get ours on pretty soon."

When Mom came to send me upstairs to bed, I pretended to be asleep, a tactic that got me a whole night in the unfinished basement to ponder the miracle of Marley's chains. Next morning was Christmas Eve and snow had stopped falling. From my half-finished basement window I saw brilliant light glance off the same new construction—speckled roofing shingles, insulation and backing mirrored and shining, the name ARMSTRONG flickering under a flawless blue winter sky, the half-finished homes looking nothing like they had the night before, their hypnotic allure under streetlamp-lit flying snow. I realized that the miracle of Marley's chains was just that—a miracle that I came to see there were no miracles—miracle that I realized imagined things had real world counterparts, that they clung to one another, unbreakable as Molloy's tire chains.

Allen shuffled in.

"Maybe Santie's not a commie," I grumbled.

"He's not?"

"Yeah—because he doesn't exist."

"Does to!"

"Santie's not a commie—but you are."

"I ain't no commie," Allen said, and shish-shushed his way over my clay tiles at remarkable speed, heading for the door. I knew Allen wasn't a commie. But I was angry at him for his inexplicable faith in Santie to fulfill his Christmas dreams, while I depended on the A-bomb to create the bottomless terror Mom and Dad may have felt in the Missile Crisis and its psychological aftereffects, which I could only hope included their splurging on my Nine Transistor.

I pursued Allen upstairs.

"I can tell if you're a commie," I said, snagged his unoccupied hand, yanked him down the hallway, and shoved him into the bathroom. I tapped the door shut, locked it, pointed to the sink. "Put your head in there." I seized him by the shoulders, forced his noggin down, freed one hand, ran water, snagged a bar of Ivory soap, and dragged it across the stiff hairs on the back of his neck. "Don't move," I whispered, took Dad's twin-blade razor in hand, swiped it across his neck, and removed a horizontal patch of hair. "I'm looking for the scar where commies implanted your brain control device."

"I'm telling Mom," he whimpered, rubbed the back of his neck, started crying, unsnapped the lock, ran out, and called, "Mom! Mom!" until I heard him find her in the distant recesses of the split-level, then the crescendo as she clomped her way toward me and appeared in the doorframe of the bathroom.

"Are you crazy?" she asked, but I didn't answer. I kept looking at her holiday apron, the flour-dusted image of Commie Claus, winking at me!

Christmas morning, Mom and Dad shish-shushed into the living room, sat on the sofa, eyes half-closed, heads together in the shape of a teepee, until Dad realized the color wheel was stuck on red, snapped up, nearly toppling Mom, and slapped the wheel into motion—yellow, blue, green, fiery red again. Seeing such a sign of life from Dad, Allen propelled himself with both arms across the ocean of carpet, knees digging deeper into the pile, until he reached the angular mound of presents at the base of the Gleam-All tree. He tore away at them, and when he found a box obviously mine kicked it aside and ravaged another. I picked up his leavings, first one from Santie, a pair of manmade neoprene oxfords, space-age pedestrian technology; then an Atomic Cape Canaveral Missile Base Set, a leviathan of a box I could scarcely grasp with both arms at full extension, its contents rattling, shifting side to side, and me with it, like a sailor on deck in a stormy sea. Lastly, amidst the utter ruin of our living room, I discovered an old Marlboro carton—Dad's smokes?—but the tag read, FROM MOM AND DAD WITH LOVE. I shot them both a look, and when they smiled from within their teepee, I knew I had them—they had a habit of disguising their best gifts in ordinary boxes. I was so sure it was my Nine Transistor that I took my time popping the lid, all the while congratulating myself for correctly psychoanalyzing my parents in the wake of the Missile Crisis. I slid the weighty device into my eager hands—a block of wood, a tuning coil, resistor with many-colored bands, a diode, stuff I'd seen in Dad's mason jar of electrical odd and ends, all soldered together with brightly coated wire—red, blue, yellow, green—oh! that metal tree! Then out the Marlboro box slid a large alligator clip and one of Dad's black Bakelite Navy headphones. I looked at Dad and Mom, saw their eyes shining out their teepee.

"What is it?" I asked them, half my mouth smiling for Mom, the other crinkled in confusion for Dad.

"A radio," Dad said.

"He made it himself, Bud," Mom added.

I studied the circuitry; they unstuck their teepee heads.

"How many transistors?" I asked.

"Doesn't need them," he replied. "No batteries, either. It's a miracle radio!"

A short while I watched Allen play with toys like other kids got, a Superman tray puzzle, Lincoln Logs, a gyroscope. When he set the gyroscope atop the puzzle box and yanked the cord it jumped out his hands and leapt onto Mom's toes. Dad repacked his cigarettes into the Marlboro carton and, as he instructed, I took the miracle radio to the half-basement and into the crawlspace. There I ventured, knees and hands, holding my flashlight, its beam jittering over old spider webs draping joists, rusted nail ends, and pale-green cinderblocks. When I reached the water lines, splotched white and turquoise, I stuck the flashlight between my knees and clamped the alligator clip to the water main. I pressed the old Navy headphone to my ear, turned the tuner slowly, and listened the way the last kid on Earth might listen for some sign of life in nuclear winter—and in that moment I felt something give. If I was the only kid alive on earth, then I could do anything. I waited to feel guilty about being the only kid alive, but I didn't. Not even the power of the A-bomb had instilled enough guilt in my parents to provide me with my dying wish, my Nine Transistor, so why should I feel guilty? No sound came from the miracle radio, and when I returned upstairs to the scene of devastation under the base of the Gleam-All tree, shredded wrapping and ribbons in Möbius strips of confounding coils about Allen's knees and shoulders, Dad asked, "You pick up anything?"

"Yeah," I said. "It's just really hard to make out."

I seized my Atomic Cape Canaveral Missile Base box, tore the tag off, FROM SANTIE—my foot!—poured its contents onto the carpet near the Gleam-All, and invested hours setting it up, ignoring the instructions, the maddening color wheel war-painting my face red, yellow, green, blue, guided only by the feeling of freedom I'd gotten in the crawlspace. Each piece snapped into place: the Missile Research Center, gantry, various launchers, a rouges' gallery of rockets, drawn straight from mythology—Thor, Atlas, Jupiter, Titan—and one other, Redstone—the rock in my David's sling. From across the vast expanse of the living room, I eyed my Goliath, the grinning Commie Claus, so satisfied by my failure in my quest for the Nine Transistor. I took the Redstone in hand, removed the Mercury capsule and replaced it with a hard-rubber nuclear warhead. I set the missile on my biggest launcher, a blue job with an eight-inch spring, and pulled it back into position, while each inch the tempered steel creaked against the plastic launch lug. When the missile clicked into place, I consulted the compass and set it due North—the Pole, of course!—then carefully adjusted the firing angle so the weapon would fly clear across the living room, dining room, to the hutch, then strike Commie Claus right between his laughing eyes. Maybe, just maybe by firing the missile across such vast, unclaimed space, by obliterating the symbol of my defeat, I thought I might claim one thing for myself, one impossible posthumous shot. I fingered the firing lever—when Allen furrowed his way to me, rolled onto his back, shrieked, "No, not Santie!" reached in, and deflected my missile into the curtains.

Less than a year later Kennedy passed and two after that Vietnam escalated, about the time Dad went with the Gemini Space Project. Allen and I were separated, got our own rooms, mine in the finished half-basement. Early January, 1966, Dad fired up the Corvair and for the first time drove us to the Brook Park Police Station, near the tennis courts and City Pool, lit only by a distant streetlamp. There, people piled their dead trees high as our split-level, then circled the heap under a new moon and starless sky. Allen stood beside me, hands stuffed deep in the pockets of his peacoat, a habit he'd developed in the process of learning what to with his wayward thumb. I remember a caravan of black dogs passed us, three pink tongues behind a panting fog, driven by a man in a long green coat, who glanced at me from beneath his broad hood. I whispered "Wait," then thought, Marley!—and wondered how he'd found the power to free himself of his chains. When a cop ignited the pile of trees, a fat woman wearing a hat like a Cossack's papakha shouted "Jesus lights the world!" and the pile burst, showered white sparks on people, shot ghost-gray smoke above, forced me back with others, while Allen remained at the very edge of the inferno, removed his hand from a pocket, and chewed on his glistening paw until Mom leapt in and hurried him back to safety.

Allen shivered once and asked me, "Santie doesn't really exist, does he?"

"Sure he does," I replied. "He was a commie. I tried to wipe him out with a nuclear warhead. You saved him, remember?"

The snapping fire cooled to orange and people inched toward it, laughing, sharing stories of how they'd survived the massive explosion.

Allen smiled, said, "Did you really think Santie was a commie?"

I watched Mom and Dad, waiting for us by the tattered nets of summer and empty City Pool encrusted with old clay-brown ice. Coals of the exhausted fire glowed so red they seemed like blood, so bloody they made the starless sky seem darker.

"I don't know," I said, and he stuffed his hand securely into his pocket.

"Just do me a favor. Next time I try to nuke Santie, you save him again, okay?" Then Allen started laughing like the others, the way you laugh when you know you should be shock-silent. "Allen," I groaned, "please!"

A KIND OF TENDER INFINITY

Just two days after John Glenn rode *Friendship 7* into orbital space, Tripp Archer came up to me in the Control Room of NASA's Supersonic Wind Tunnel. He fell to one knee, smack dab in front of me, ready to propose marriage.

A few feet away, my sister, Clytie May, leaned against a burnished metal maze of gauges and switches. Her bleary, self-satisfied eyes locked on mine. Her horn-rimmed face gloated, framed like John Glenn's behind the visor of his space helmet. She reached back and adjusted her copper hairclip shaped like a tuning coil, as if ready to broadcast Tripp's proposal to the Free World. She snickered, hand over mouth, under the aegis of being my psychic sister, believing she'd predicted Tripp would be down on one knee before me within a year. But she missed the part about how he'd drop in the wind tunnel.

The tunnel itself was shut down, yet Tripp himself wobbled on his knee like he was inside the ten-by-ten test section, blasted by Mach 3 air molecules across his quivering, scarcely aerodynamic frame.

"Will you—" Tripp paused and nudged the slide rule on his belt. It flopped from his hip and hung loose between his legs, a little to the left, a rather shocking angle. I almost laughed, not to hurt him, but because my sister seemed to enjoy refereeing the whole affair, while I held a donut in one hand, blazing black coffee in the other, and under my left armpit squeezed a half-foot high stack of keypunch cards I had to run for Mr. Rice, Engineering Supervisor of the Fission Power Group.

"Jesus, Tripp," I said, but all I could think was how, even after sidling right to block him from Clytie May's view, I'd failed to conceal his dolorous knee-drop. Then Mr. Rice entered the control room, too. Clytie May was the Lewis Research Center's receptionist and had been dating Mr. Rice six weeks, so I was certain she'd acquainted him with her so-called psychic powers—and my love life.

Clytie May pushed off the control panel and seemed to dance, a subtle victory shake of her hips that resembled a strange connubial ritual. A spot of hot coffee slopped onto my wrist and I winced, which of course manifested itself in a reflex wince in my suitor's eyes, thinking I'd tacitly rejected him without hearing the question. He shuddered. His slide rule shivered.

"Muh, marry me?" sputtered from Tripp's lips, but all I could think was how to prove to Clytie May that her clairvoyance was a lot of hooey. You didn't need a psychic to see that one woman with a two-year degree in FORTRAN, working with twenty-three assorted NASA engineers, all of whom logged many unheralded hours in space between their ears, was going to get at least one proposal. Still, I was surprised. I'd only officially dated Tripp three times, our first the unveiling of a new Titan booster, second the NASA summer picnic at Euclid Park, lovely, except the beach was closed, polluted, unsafe to swim. Our last date was an airshow over Cleveland Public Square, featuring a 2.6-second flyover by the Blue Angles and a triple sonic boom that visibly shook windows in the higher floors of the Terminal Tower.

Westfall, the new aeronautical engineer, whom Clytie May called Zephyr Guy, came in to warm up the wind tunnel. Its compressor groaned a few revolutions and slowly rose in volume, like a mechanical *Bolero*.

I tried to speak over the pulsating crescendo.

TRIPP! I'LL HAVE TO THINK ABOUT IT!

I'm not sure he heard me. If he had, I'd not have known it. He looked the same as ever: dark hair, early male-pattern balding, black eyeglass rims that formed a kind of venerable porch, under which half his mouth smiled warmly, endearingly really, and the other half sat in a flat line, like the perfect seam in the new Mercury Capsule separation ring they were testing in the big NASA hangar.

Tripp spoke out the flat side of his mouth.

ALRIGHT!

Then, somewhere in the jumble of wind-tunnel noise, something came out the warm side.

I WILL MAKE YOU HAPPY!

At which point Mr. Rice spoke to Zephyr Guy, waited until he shut the compressor down, then stood by Clytie May, both in anticipation of something more from me.

"I'll let you know by the end of the day," I told Tripp.

"Work day?" he said out the flat side of this mouth.

"Right. Five," I said, which seemed to satisfy his need.

Despite it being our lunch hour, Clytie May hovered in the doorframe of my office, blocking any attempt I may make to escape.

I stalled. Made busy. Tapped papers into neat stacks, set them down, then pushed the stacks around my desk.

My eyes landed on Tripp's latest NASA technical report, #MD-61-7, resting under my coffee mug, a half-moon brown stain under the title like a faint happy face. Tripp wanted me to read it. First time he'd asked me to read anything. I'll admit, I was looking forward to it. I didn't know what I wanted, seldom thought about marrying anyone, but I wanted to understand the mysteries of space travel. How one really does it. How you blast into the unknown with only a hope you'll come back to the known. I wanted what these NASA guys had. I wanted in. But I didn't how to get in. I wanted some higher purpose. Something. Anything but my sister's Dark-Ages divinations.

Clytie May stuck her head in my doorway.

"I'm glad to be right about Tripp," she said. "I mean, I'm happy for you. But why did he propose to you in the wind tunnel?"

"Maybe because last month, after he presented me with that Sputnik brooch, all you had to say to him is, 'Nice. Predictable. Another reminder that the Russians are always at our heels.' Now Tripp spends our time together trying to be unpredictable."

I told Clytie May that last week, while she was out with Mr. Rice, Tripp showed up at our apartment. I was into a nice new bag of Fritos when Tripp produced a book of poems he'd gotten at a London bookstore while at a conference called *Nuclear Design for Space Travel and World Peace.* He held forth with *The Marriage of Heaven and Hell.* Strange language flew past his lips.

> *Rintrah roars and shakes his fires in the burden'd air;*
> *Hungry clouds swag on the deep!*

The Fritos went soggy in my immobilized mouth.

"What did you do?" Clytie May said, the same hypnotic glaze over her eyes when she watched her soap, *The Secret Storm.*

"I told him to stop it."

Clytie May sanded the sides of her nose with both hands, a habit I deplored since I knew she was erasing a smile. While Clytie May's horn-rims bounced under her fingers, the floor began to rumble, another brief test of the new RP-1 engine for the Titan booster. That instant it looked as if Clytie May herself were lifting off into the poet's "burden'd air." When they throttled the test engine back, the rumbling subsided to a vibration, then a mere thought, the way you know the Earth is spinning, latitude-adjusted, about eight-hundred miles an hour, but you don't feel it. It's physics so pure you can't feel it. You can only know it in your mind.

When the engine test stopped, Clytie May dropped her hands and revealed her triumphant red nose.

"Dear," she laughed, "he was reading a *marriage* poem to you and you act so surprised that he proposed?"

"*That* was a marriage poem?"

"Right," Clytie May insisted. "I'll go with you to the courthouse for the license," she said. "I'll show you how. I've been through it before."

"Show me what?" I said. "How to be married *and* divorced?"

I guess I was getting cranky since, after her divorce, Clytie May'd moved into my place on Cedar Point Road near the Rocket Engine Test Facility. She kept calling our cramped apartment the Gemini Capsule, and laughed, the way people laugh off something that's too true. She hoisted her mammoth purse a couple inches and clamped it to one side, like she was smashing atoms in the surface of the glossy green alligator hide. She put on her sad, all-knowing divorcée smile, one that drew lines like Martian canals at the corners of her eyes and made her look tired. "Oh," swan-dove from her lower lip and I softened a moment, but then came back.

"You didn't predict anything about Tripp and me," I said. "Anyone could see one of these NASA guys would eventually pop the question. It's a statistical probability. Could have been Zephyr Guy for all I know."

I softened again. Felt damn guilty. Tripp was a nice guy, more than a statistic. Always up to something. Kind. Polite. Even caring. I may have accepted his proposal on the spot if not for Clytie May, so smart, so sure, so now recovered from her little death-diving 'Oh.'

"Dear," Clytie May said solemnly, "I worry about you. If we're taking odds, I didn't think they were in your favor. You're almost thirty. It was only my reading your palm that convinced me you'd get a proposal at all." I stared at my mutinous right palm. "I mean you're shy. And look at these men. They're in the *space* program. Know what mean?"

I knew what she meant. Tripp, himself, was working on compact, lightweight nuclear power plants for deep space travel, a means to survive years en route to far-off planets. He worked a lot. With each FORTRAN run I made for Tripp, each slap of six-inch high stacks of output on his desk, I swore I could see the beachhead of his brow recede. I could not begin to imagine how one solved a problem like that. Deep space travel. I was convinced he'd not solve it before he'd lost hair everywhere on his body, and strangely begin to devolve into a hairless infant, a rather ghastly supposition in light of his marriage proposal.

"Do you even care about Tripp's future?" I asked Clytie May. "Maybe I'm wrong for him."

"I can read his palm," Clytie May pleaded. "Why don't you call him over?"

"Are you nuts? What will he think? I'm supposed to be *seriously* weighing his proposal."

"Then if you could just bring me some object of his…"

I fingered the Sputnik brooch on my sweater.

"This?" I said without really thinking, a remnant reflex from our childhood, times Clytie May conscripted me to search through our parents' dresser drawers for brooches, rings, cufflinks and such so she could lay hands on them and presage whether their marriage would last. I said it wouldn't. She said it would. It didn't.

"No," Clytie May scolded. "The object has to be something intimate, something really important to Tripp, like his life depended on it."

I swear my eyes turned only a millisecond to Tripp's report #MD-61-7, then shot back to Clytie May's eternally vigilant eyeballs.

I tried to change the subject.

"Clytie May, do you want to get lunch or what?" I asked, and prodded a stack of keypunch cards to cover Tripp's report.

When I rose from my chair, she floated slowly down, landed in my seat, and crossed her legs. "*Zero gravity,*" she said with malicious delight, snatched up Tripp's report, and added, "This'll do."

The gray, riveted underbelly of a Boeing 707 grumbled low over my red Corvair. Huge heat snakes shimmered behind its four pendulous engines. I had the Corvair running, heater on high.

"TWA!" Clytie May claimed, part of our childhood game to identify the airline only by the plane's underside. We were parked at Cleveland Hopkins Airport, same spot our parents often brought us when we were kids, before their divorce. Clytie May still insisted on coming here for lunch, even in Cleveland winters. "See, I told you," she went on, as the airliner whistled to a stop at its gate. "TWA." Her upper lip disappeared into her tuna salad on rye. I shivered and stuck five curled fingers to my car's heat vent.

"LOOK!" I said, my voice suddenly competing with a DC-8 scorching overhead. "I ONLY HAVE UNTIL FIVE TO FIGURE THIS TRIPP THING OUT!" Then blessed silence, part of our crazy up and down volumetric dialogue at Hopkins. "And you're not helping."

Clytie May stuck her arm out, limp. It hung in the air like a gangway, inviting me to come aboard. "Give me your hand," she whispered, "and I'll see what your palm tells us. Just to confirm my earlier reading."

I could feel the muscle reflex in my forearm urging my hand forward, but I resisted, one of the only times. In the past she'd whine, "What have you got to lose? You don't believe in psychic powers, anyway."

A VC10 thundered over.

"BUT DOESN'T THE NOISE INTERFERE WITH YOUR READING?"

"No," she said. "The only thing that interferes is a smarty-pants like you."

"Clytie May, you can't give me one instance of your predicting anything."

"I knew we would be going to the Moon."

"Baloney. Everyone knew Kennedy was going to make that speech."

"Alright, then. Do you remember Dr. Boem visiting NASA from South Korea?" Clytie May waited until I nodded. "Well, when Mr. Rice introduced him to me, I shook Dr. Boem's hand and suddenly smelled a terrible stench. At first I thought it was his body odor. It was so puzzling. He seemed so nicely dressed. So, I explained to Dr. Boem that I was a psychic. He smiled, and when I described the nauseating odor to him, he explained that he had been present at the firebombing of Tokyo in 1945 and never forgot the odor of bodies no one had time to bury."

It was American Airlines' turn to drown me out.

"OR MAYBE HE JUST HAD B.O., CLYTIE MAY!" I said.

"ALRIGHT!" she replied. "Hand me Tripp's report."

She took the blue-covered NASA technical report, closed her eyes, and ran her right hand smoothly over the surface, almost lovingly, as you would a rare silk or satin, something arousing. Her nostrils flared, eyebrows twitched, and she had me quite believing that even if she weren't a bona fide psychic, she believed deeply that she was, believed it with a kind of scary faith I feared I would never find.

"I'm not getting anything," she shrugged.

"No?" I stammered, then felt like a buffoon for my momentary lapse into disappointment.

"MAYBE IF YOU READ SOME OF IT!" she said.

I waited until the next jet landed, found my opening, then held forth.

Consider the following one-dimensional boron lump. At any given energy the directional fluxes incident at the boron interfaces are B+ and B-…

"No good," Clytie May grunted, her eyes still sealed shut. "I'm trying to tune into the future, sis." The tuning coil hairclip atop her head seemed to hum. "Skip to Tripp's conclusion," she said, and I went on.

> *Three forms for g(E) have been obtained. The one obtained from P-1 Blackness Theory is perhaps on a better theoretical foundation…*

I tossed the report in back, put the Corvair in reverse, and pulled away from the airport fence. "We have to get back to work," I told her, and crammed the stick into first gear. "You get anything from *that*, Clytie May?"

"Yep. It means you and Tripp will be very happy together."

"Happy? How? I don't understand a word of it, even the conclusion."

"So, he's a deep guy."

"Deep isn't the word. And what in hell is 'Blackness Theory?'"

I ground the Corvair into third, punched it, fishtailed on a plate of ice, then quickly knocked it into fourth.

"Fair enough, but some marriages are based on mystery," she said. "Besides, he'll give you brilliant children."

A brief, high-pitched whistle emerged from my mouth like an F-4 Phantom taxying to take off. "I-I-i-i-i…don't know, Clytie May."

My god, I wondered. Would Tripp want children?

You keypunch FORTRAN IV long enough, you wonder if buried deep in code is a kind of key to complexities of the human heart, as if the right concatenation of commands will reveal some single solution. Some people doodled. I keypunched:

```
10      IF (MARRIAGE .NE. ME)
20      GOTO 30
30      THE SINGLE SOLUTION
40      PAUSE
50      CALL ANY GUY I WANT
60      DO HIM
        EXIT
        END
```

I stacked the keypunch cards like I was ready to take them to the reader. It was fun to pretend. The clock over Tripp's door read 4:47 p.m. when I saw Clytie May go into his office, heard the hum of their two voices, then saw her exit with her goofy omniscient grin, pretending I wasn't aware of her. I tore my keypunch cards in pieces, gave chase, and caught her in the wind tunnel at the water fountain.

"What did you say to Tripp?"

Instead of answering me, she bent over the fountain and pressed the bar. A little stream of water bubbled over her lips, then she straightened up, wiped her mouth. "I told Tripp that your indecisiveness should not hurt his feelings," she said. "I said I was a psychic and that even if you say no, eventually you will say yes."

"Clytie May," I said. "You're so interested in Tripp, why don't YOU MARRY HIM!"

"You don't have to shout," she whispered, like silence was a kind of sacred retort. She started fussing with her hair, fluffing and flattening it around her tuning coil. I was so mad, I dashed into Tripp's office. He was sitting at his desk, slide rule flat in front of him, its hairline cursor set to π, eyeglasses high on his forehead. He looked at me. I looked at him, then realized it was the first I'd seen his eyes unobstructed by the coke-bottle lenses of his glasses. I stood spellbound by what I saw there, a kind of tender infinity, like π itself.

But then I blurted, "I'm sorry, Tripp. I'll have to let you know tomorrow."

He didn't say anything, just nudged the hairline off π.

After work, the short ride to our apartment, Clytie May was silent, the only sound my Corvair jittering over February potholes. When we got inside, Clytie May rattled a Jiffy Pop pan over the electric burner until the top rose, steaming, pregnant with exploded kernels. She crash-landed in our too-large-for-the-place sofa, tore open the aluminum dome, and poked a few popped kernels in her mouth while others tumbled to her lap. Then we watched *Ten Little Indians* on television. Ten strangers are invited and assemble at a mansion on an isolated mountaintop. They are told that one of them has caused the death of an innocent person, and then one by one they get knocked off, presumably by one of the ten in their group. We were only few minutes into the show and Clytie May spoke.

"It's Mike Raven," she said. "He's the killer. What a playboy."

She followed shortly with:

"It's gotta be that William Blore, the private dick."

And then:

"Alright, my final prediction. It's that Ann Clyde. No one who looks that young and innocent can actually be so."

I hated this. Clytie May did it all the time.

"Clytie May, you can't keep saying so-and-so did it and then change to another so-and-so. You have to stick with one suspect."

"Why?"

"Don't you have a milligram of sense in you? You can't predict everything will happen because everything can't happen. Which one do you think did it?"

"I don't prognosticate well under pressure," she said and wrapped her arms tight about the Jiffy Pop pan.

Over at NASA, the Titan engine test began, a full 470-second burst, from which they'd estimate the burnout velocity of the rocket. I went to the picture window, saw the lights of the test hangar, clouds shaped like a cornucopia roiling out the colossal exhaust pipe. The sound of a Convair 880 jet joined the Titan, screeched down at Hopkins.

"CLYTIE MAY," I said. "YOU CHEAT!"

"You're shouting again. And I know you're putting Tripp off just to spite me."

So I was, and so she went on rapid-fire, ignoring my *Ten Little Indians* accusation, soothsaying like mad while I stood silent.

"Don't you see, sis? We'll all be great friends living in the space age."

"While you and Tripp rocket through outer space, I'll travel through psychic inner space, from past to present—to infinity."

"Hey, I'll join the diplomatic corps. I'll figure out Khrushchev's state secrets from a single handshake."

Clytie May went on like that, while I wondered in which world of genetics such a creature could actually be my sister. Assuming she was, shouldn't I have some undiscovered psychic ability? I braced myself against the window sill, searched the sky for my own answers, winter stars spread every which way.

Nothing came. And Clytie May continued.

"You and Tripp will live in a nice split-level with three bedrooms."

"In a suburb with a natural, earthy name, like Rocky River or Olmstead Falls."

"Two children, both with music lessons at very early ages."

"You'll trade your red Corvair in for a nice station wagon."

"A Rambler, I think. Yeah, a Rambler."

"Saturday nights, I'll babysit while you and Tripp take in a movie. Hey, have you guys seen *The Misfits*?"

It seemed I was marrying everything but Tripp. Titans, jumbo jets, station wagons, Clark Gables, Marilyn Monroes. As Clytie May rambled, rumblings of the Titan test got under the foundation of our apartment, traveled all directions, seemed to shake the entire planet under Kennedy's Moon, to take on an eerie, shivering sound of truth, the way truth can simply be everything that ever was or will be. I searched the cold, star-strewn sky again, but had no inkling of my future or Tripp's. I wondered, if I was marrying everything, who was it marrying me? And what would I be called? Mrs. Everything? Then I found a star, low in the east, one not part of any constellation I knew, no Castor, no Pollux, no name I was aware of, no brave myth to call its own. I realized the starlight I saw may have shone hundreds of years before my seeing it, that this star may in fact, in its part of the universe, be dead and dark. In a little while, when Clytie May shushed, the Titan engine ramping up, I would call her to the window with me, to try her powers again, to see if this unnamed light, so near, so real, may be dead. Or not. I hoped tomorrow I would have an answer for Tripp. Whether yes or no. But for now, while the world trembled below, while aboard our little Gemini, just seconds to burnout, all that mattered is that I could see this single light—distant, lonely, momentary. There you are, I thought. There you are.

WE WANDERED OURSELVES
BACK TO ONE

I'm just as much a Daoist as the next guy, so when I saw Amos yammering on his cell phone, and Wolf Man, mind someplace else, both standing at the ass-end of the new shit-sucker truck the county loaned us to keep up with our under-capacity sewage plant, designed for 250 people, now serving 399—when I heard the queerest groaning of the vacuum pump, saw the pressure gauge on the tank rise clean into the red zone, well, my *wu-wei* kicked in. The two knuckleheads who supposedly worked for me deserved a good dose of *wu-wei*, demanded it, really, and I decided to follow that holy path of non-action and let, in that moment before whatever will happen, well, happen.

It was the sort of moment that just about prefigures, configures, and confounds the very nature of our existence, to let the shit fly or not to let the shit fly, that tick before the rain of human excrement exited the top of the trembling shit-sucker through the so-called, patent-pending, patently ironic, 'safety' valve.

When it blew, it was, it was, like a shit trumpet heralding in a new era of non-interference, Amos's and Wolf Man's chins stuck skyward, pointed directly under the wellspring of crap in a kind of unselfconscious reverence of the fateful fount, a millisecond before realizing what shit goes up must come down, and it did, with both hollering, "Truth!"

Because that's my name—Truth Thomas.

Young Amos, posture like a comma, suddenly straightened into an exclamation point and raced for the village pickup with Wolf Man loping close behind, wiping crap from his gray *canis lupus* Vandyke.

"Hey!" I hollered. "You ain't stinking up an official vehicle of the incorporated Village of Luckey. Run home, shower off, then get back here and clean this up!"

Once they were out of sight, I strategically traversed the area of devastation, foreswore my *wu-wei* a couple seconds to shut the truck down, then noticed Ghost's community burgers cooking, a small pillow of smoke rising a few streets down on Perry. Well, I took the village pickup and got myself over there because what's the use of going to all the trouble of being a Daoist if you've no chance to tell someone of the fruits of such philosophical labor, namely a good story of letting shit fly.

When I got out front of Ghost's place, more smoke rose from the old boy's backyard, filled limbs of the black walnut lurching and brooding over the back eaves of his house. Then the smoke rolled forward in a kind of carcinogenic fog across Ghost's brown sagging roof.

I followed the burger fog to Ghost's backyard, where the bald, white-bearded old goat, already stoned on Old Rip Van Winkle whiskey, lolled in his chaise. He pumped the accordion his wife'd given him before she died, young, tragically, the kind of passing that set old Ghost to ride the rails, then join the Merchant Marines, get torpedoed thrice in three different Liberty Ships, his oily ass hauled out the North Atlantic three times, a Lazarus-like hat trick that got him the name Ghost. I suspected his was a life so full of *action* it drove him to drink a goodly portion of the government pension he got from Congress when they eventually realized those poor bastards had been sitting ducks for Hitler's U-boats.

"Why don't you give that groanbox a rest?" I said.

Ghost set the instrument back and tried to rise from his chaise, pile-driving his elbows into the plastic armrests, working his legs like a turtle on its back.

I let him try awhile. My *wu-wei*, of course. He never managed.

"Well, hello there, Truth!" Ghost called.

"Yeah," I said, "well, Truth says you're loaded."

He was relieved then, free from the pretentious courtesy of rising to meet me. He nodded behind himself in the direction of the smoking Weber grill.

"Flip them burgers, will you?"

I went over and rattled the lid of the grill so he could hear it. But I didn't lift it. I just pretended to flip his burgers, and served him right, sitting there, plugged into the nineteen-thirties while someone else took care of the here and now. No thanks. Besides, I knew he wanted me to come back, say, "Man, those are big burgers." But I'd already seen the burgers before. Weighty affairs, around a pound each. They always numbered twelve, same as Christ's disciples, intentional on Ghost's part, burgers he called his apostles, the combustive products of which spread the good word in our village of a free meal. Now, in the Year of Our Lord 2015, any hungry pilgrim was welcome to the massive burgers. Mostly kids, neighbors, and dogs got his burgers, though once an older woman, an outsider to Luckey, in a green paper hat and a sash that read MISS WOBBLIE 1937, came by, ate two, and kissed Ghost's bald spot while he slumbered in one of his Van Winkle-stupors.

Whatever. Who was I to interfere in God's work? So I pretended to flip his burgers, a right-Dao thing to do.

"Big, ain't they?" Ghost mumbled after hearing me set the spatula back. "I'll take it from here."

I started to tell him about the shit-sucker blowing all over Amos and Wolf Man, but he got that hobo grin on his face, retrieved his groanbox, and started in with one of his hobo verses he repeated over and over before his pickled memory would allow him to skip to the next one.

> *Why don't you work like other folks do?*
> *How the hell can I work when there ain't no work to do?*
> *Hallelujah, I'm a bum.*
> *Hallelujah, bum again.*
> *Hallelujah, give us a hand—*

He paused and looked up at me.

"I'm *The One*, right?" he said, referring to his favorite Jet Li film in which he kills 122 alternative-universe versions of himself to grow infinitely stronger.

"Yeah," I replied. "You *The One*."

Ghost started to stretch his hand out to me, then nodded, closed his eyes over his milky-blue cataracts and, like Wolf Man and Amos, moments before the shit-trumpet sounded, old Ghost's mind was off somewhere else, hoboing his head off, riding rails, no man telling him what to do or be, polite as can be, sober as need be, and it gave me just the slightest shiver of *wu-wei* guilt, what I let happen to Wolf Man and Amos back at the shit-sucker. Well, at least sorry for Wolf Man. Unlike Ghost, I'd no idea where young Amos's mind had been, guessed it captive in the guts of his cell phone. But it'd only been a week since Wolf Man lost his fourteen Iditarod-in-training huskies to the County Humane Society on account of his bringing the dogs with him from Fairbanks to our fair Village of Luckey to care for his sister after she crashed her car and paralyzed herself waist-down while texting:

FUD…DILLIGAS?

Which I later learned, after consulting Amos's twelve-year-old niece, meant:

Fear, Uncertainty, Disinformation…Do I Look Like I Give A Shit?

The county woman and sheriff said that many dogs was too many for one man, not enough room, came, packed Wolf Man's majestic, blue-and-brown-eyed athletes into a cramped trailer, and hauled them away. So that was where Wolf Man's head'd been at the shit-sucker. Had to be. Alaska. Mind-mushing. Drifting snow buffeting his sled. Scintillating powder bursting left and right in cold sunlight, tops of snow-crusted green pines sawtoothing a pale Arctic sky, the pull of his dogs, each to a single purpose, always forward, muscle and speed blended to win the greatest race on Earth.

Fuck. Wolf Man loved those dogs, and when he'd returned to Luckey fed them salmon, while he and his sister subsisted on ramen noodles.

"I'm going to kill myself," Wolf Man told me, and that's when I asked him to work for me, which seemed to persuade him to remain with the living a little while longer. It left me feeling decent and all, but also a little embarrassed for not following the *wu-wei*, not interfering. I mean, there must be a balance to things. Planets turn about the Sun. Moons turn about the planets. Folks ought to go on with their lives peacefully, predictably. Who would ask Venus to abandon its orbit of the Sun to help out Mars, risking the whole cosmic balance of things? Only, this whole balance of things was sometimes tricky when shit was always happening.

Ghost's burgers sizzled and hissed at me, a hostile audience to my thoughts. His eyes closed, and he dropped his groanbox to the ground. I picked it up, set it back on his lap, and pressed two fingertips to his wrist.

"Jesus, Mary, and Joseph!" he said, eyes still closed. "I ain't dead yet."

He mumbled something, eyes popping open, caught hold of some new scrap of hobo memories. I could tell. He shushed me, though I wasn't saying anything, then listened briefly for a response in chorus to his last line, *Hallelujah, give us s hand—*, and when none came, skipped to a new verse.

"Here's one for you," he told me, "boss man."

> *Whenever I get all the money I earn,*
> *The boss will be broke, and to work must turn.*
> *Hallelujah, I'm a bum,*
> *Hallelujah, bum again!*

So accused of being boss man, I thought back to the rain of shit that morning on Wolf Man and Amos, thought maybe the *wu-wei* was so cosmically mysterious that I couldn't see the benefit of not saving those two, like, perhaps by allowing the shit to fly on those knuckleheads I accidently and simultaneously created teamwork based on a common goal—those two to stop loafing and get to a shower fast. Or I may have tacitly and nonviolently inspired them to pay attention when I said, "This here is a *pressure gauge*. Watch it closely!"

Some days, it was harder than ever to go with the flow, but I was determined. I understood Wolf Man's Walter-Mittyian mind flights. In my younger days, before I embraced the *wu-wei*—or it embraced me—I was an anarchist, and for years after pined for those chaotic moments when I challenged the establishment. The big protest in San Francisco in 1971, Vietnam War Out Now! Good times, except when I got my head busted open, not by pigs, but by some tripping freak with a paisley headband who thought I was Jesus and tried to nail me to a park bench.

"Come on, man," he said, "die for everyone!"

God, I fucking hate paisley.

Like Jesus, I suppose, I was a rabble-rouser back then. But I wanted to do Him one better. I'd read my anarchists, Bakunin, Kropotkin, wanted to best both those fellows, too, by being against everything, even against people forming groups to be against everything, which left me hopelessly alone, broke, in rehab, and eventually shipped back to Luckey, all expenses paid by my mom, God rest her soul, who got me this job as Head of Village Maintenance.

So, I maintain—or try.

When I first got back from the West Coast, I thought maybe I could start my own brand of small-town anarchy. You know, on a smaller scale. Something I could manage.

I started the Anarchist's Club of Luckey. I ran off flyers on an old Ditto machine. I loved the pale purple type, the fragrant solvent, wet drying pages. And how cheap it all was. I posted my announcement in the U.S. Post Office.

CALLING ALL ANARCHISTS OF LUCKEY, OHIO
FIRST MEETING NOON, MAY 15, 2015
TRUTH'S PLACE
BE ON TIME

Fuck. Rookie mistakes.

I secretly saw our Postmaster, Sighrus Heeving, tear it down and expertly jump-shoot my crumpled flyer into the wastebasket, grumbling, "Not in my patch of America."

No one showed on time—or any time.

That was when I found the *wu-wei* at a library sidewalk sale, *Dao for Everyday—something or other*, fifteen cents.

No more getting almost crucified. No more flipping behemoth burgers. Just a faith that there were mysteries of the cosmos, its checks and balances, so to speak, that I couldn't begin to understand. So why try?

I left Ghost chortling about hobo days and walked out front of his place. I saw his burger smoke sailing down Perry toward Main Street. It kind of relaxed me, the way smoke can slosh in a slight wind like water, rock a soul to rest.

I was really in the flow of things when I saw Trudy B's new Toro burst through Ghost's burger smog and charge down Perry Street toward where it dead-ended in a fifteen-foot deep irrigation ditch. The Toro was a push-button starting, self-mulching, self-tuning, self-adjusting, and how ever many selves a lawnmower like that can have. Self-propelled, too. Stuck on one of the higher speeds. Amos had wound a bread tie about the engine brake so Trudy B could walk away, leave the engine running and, apparently, the beast in gear, which Trudy B'd assuredly done, while she went off on one of her mind vacations. She stood there, young, pretty, the way baby fat never quite leaves some faces, even after thirty-three years, fingers over her mouth, watching the Toro.

I supposed I could have rushed over and untwisted that bread tie. But what the unnatural mechanical creature had to do with the cosmic balance of things, I didn't know or care.

Just as I stopped pondering the matter, the Toro flung itself into the farmer's milky phosphate-polluted ditchwater, where it gurgled, snorted once, then died, I swear, with an olé!

Trudy B and I got to the ditch, looked down at her dead Toro. She didn't say anything, hadn't the slightest idea I could have stopped the machine.

I was sure she thought it was her fault, entirely. People used the "B" in reference to Trudy's last name, to stand for "Believer." She didn't seem to mind. Trudy's being the "Believer" wasn't religious or anything. Well, maybe. She believed in the infallibility of industrial corporate America. Take the predecessor to the suicidal Toro, some other name brand or other, how many times I'd called Amos over there with me to help her start it.

Trudy B'd say, "I'm sorry. It must be something *I* did. It's only a year and three days old."

Three days past the warranty.

Young Amos'd scratch his head.

"I think it's pretty much dead."

"No," Trudy B'd sob, "it's got to be something *I* did."

And so it was like that with her. Self-reproach. Guilt. Belief.

I realized I was almost proud of Trudy B, the way she'd simply let the hell-bent bull run itself to destruction. I felt like recruiting her into the *wu-wei*, only that would take me out of my natural orbit. She needed to find the *wu-wei* in her own way. Still, I had a smidge of remorse—or curiosity.

"I'm sorry," I said with a somber face.

She pulled fingers away from her mouth and, before I could say anything more, said:

"When my boss fired me, she bought me a ticket to an A's game. She wanted me to come along with other non-fired people from the office. Why would she do that?"

Well, I knew the story of Trudy B's being fired, but the A's ticket was a new wrinkle, and likely the reason the marauding mower'd gotten lose from her believing fingertips in the first place.

"You mean," I started slowly, "that job you had in San Francisco five years ago, before you had to come back here to Luckey and live with your mother?"

"What else?"

Indeed, Trudy B'd lived and worked in the kingdom of West Coast pinstripes, twenty-ninth floor of a spanking new, earthquake-resistant monument to management's ego overlooking the blue, pimpled San Francisco Bay, until they discovered that her subordinates were selling cocaine through the interoffice mail. Aside from her workers being epically stupid, Trudy B was let go on account of, "She should have known" what they were up to.

Like I said, I could have introduced her to the *wu-wei*, but wondered if that alone would ever snap the umbilical cord she had to her bougie Frisco past.

"I never even tried pot, let alone cocaine," she said.

"And now?" I said, trying to make a little time. She was pretty.

"What's your deal, anyway?" she said, then steamed and ooooed, trembling like the shit-sucker just before the shit-trumpet sounded.

I put on my cell and left a message for Wolf Man to pull her Toro out of the ditch, but he didn't answer, so I headed back to the sewage plant to check on my worker bees.

Well, those two were just fine. They'd hosed down the shit-stained gravel. They started the wood chipper, then one of those crotch rockets zoomed past, its two-cycle *ying-ying-ying!* dopplering away. Right behind and creaking came Luckey's finest, Fayteh Mann, our work/study cop from college, in his Chevy Cavalier cruiser, top speed about eighty, his hunk-a-junk straining so hard I swear it sounded like *yang-yang-yang*, and I had to wonder, being a Daoist and such, if Fayteh's *yang-yang-yang* ever caught the rocket's *ying-ying-ying*, if some new, peaceful order would emerge in our troubled village, one in which I'd never feel the need to interfere in anything. But Fayteh didn't stand a chance. He screeched to a stop a little past us, got out, shaded his eyes, and watched the rocket the way Wiley Coyote might, while Roadrunner became a harlequin-smile, then speck in the distance.

Fayteh reversed all the way back to the sewage plant, got out, and walked up to me, like I was manning a cop complaint counter, like I could or would do anything about anything.

"Did you fucking see that?"

"Yeah," I said. "Fast little shit. Why don't you just give up?"

Fayteh was about to respond, when a call buzzed in, Wolf Man's paralyzed sister, Ellie, saying Wolf Man was on the roof of their ranch "and he's gonna jump!"

Anyway, I promised Fayteh a fuller consideration of his hopelessly pursuing the crotch-rocket, then got down to Wolf Man's place, where he was on the roof, on all fours, at one of the front eaves. About an eight-foot drop, but only three feet above a tall, lush, densely foliated taxus bush.

Wolf Man shouted down at us:

"Years I've been living, eating, shitting, breathing—freezing with those animals!"

He reached back and rapidly scratched one of his hindquarters.

"I can see that," I said, thinking fleas.

I felt someone tap my leg and say, "Truth."

"What?"

It was Ellie, parked behind me in a wheelchair.

I liked her. She had a twinkle in her eye despite the hair missing from the right half of her scalp, a peppering of follicles beginning to reclaim the foibles of cell phone technology.

"Focus," she said.

"I'll try," I replied.

"No, you don't get it. FOCUS. Fuck Off Cuz Ur Stupid."

At first I thought she might have developed a rare form of Tourette's that manifested itself in only acronyms.

"Just kidding," she said and smiled out the unscorched side of her face.

I was glad. In Ellie's laidback humor, I felt I may have a kindred spirit in the *wu-wei*, so I blurted out to Wolf Man, who was by then crouching, ready to spring:

"Wolfie," I said. "Whatever!"

And he lunged from the eaves, instantly crashing into the taxus. He lay there, limbs akimbo with those of the bush.

His horrified sister beat my legs with her fists.

"What's the matter with you!"

I guessed I was wrong about Ellie being ready for the *wu-wei*.

When Wolf Man emerged from the bush, he was creeping on all fours, head down, like a penitent dog.

"There, there," I said. "Good boy."

He gave a sheepish smile, strange for the Wolf Man, and I knew, taxus scratches aside, he was okay.

"I didn't think he'd do it," I said to Ellie, and she was about to get way up in my *wu-wei*, when I saw that Wolf Man's unsuccessful leap of desperation had caught the attention of Trudy B, who arrived at the scene, saying, "Somehow, I think this is my fault," referring to the night Wolf Man wandered onto her front lawn howling like a lunatic about his lost Iditarod dogs and, so she said, she doused the lights, dead-bolted her door, and pretended to not be there.

"Wolf Man needed one of those interventions," she said, shiny-eyed. "He needed me, and I shut him out."

Ellie rolled her wheelchair over the toes of Trudy B's right foot.

"Oh, sorry," Ellie said, gruesomely half-grinning on the scarred side of her face.

Satisfied that Ellie had transferred her anger from me to Trudy B, I packed Wolf Man into the village pickup and drove back to the wood chipper.

When we got there, Amos was feeding the chipper. Next to me in the pickup, Wolf Man was mushing again, somewhere between Anchorage and Nome. I thought about loaning my *Dao for Everyday—something or other* to him. And to Trudy B. Maybe it would help them. Maybe they would be happier not going off in their heads to Alaska, San Francisco, far corners of everywhere. What was the point of leaving Luckey, only to have the world kick you back again and again? It was better to stay put, to find some still point inside yourself and plant your restless ass in the *wu-wei*.

My shift was almost over. I was thinking, at last, everything'd settled nicely into a right-Dao day, the way all the mild calamities were being washed by the cosmic flow of things into a valley of forgotten travails. My thoughts drifted to the *wu-wei*. I felt centered.

I got out and settled back against the door of the pickup, felt the quiescence of the cosmos not ten seconds when Amos started jamming tree limbs into the loud metallic maw of the wood chipper too fast. His pant leg caught on the branch of an ash. The chipper chomped, began to drag the limb closer into tree-oblivion, also dragging Amos by his pant cuff along, leaping like a terrified ballerina performing an échappé sauté.

All the while Amos and his pant leg were inexorably headed into the wood chipper, I wondered how I knew the French for "escape leap," mind-fucked on the ballerina I'd dated who dumped the old drug-addled me in Haight-Ashbury one night, I mean, literally dumped me there.

"Hey!" Amos pleaded, glancing at tundra-trekking Wolf Man, then me.

I looked to nature, the jet-streaked sky, gurgling filthy water in the irrigation ditch, anything in nature's cosmic arsenal to tell me what to do. Finally—I sprung for Amos's leg and snatched him from the eager teeth of the wood chipper.

"Thanks," Amos said and rolled to his feet like he'd merely taken a tumble in tackle football.

"Whatever," I said.

I didn't know how to explain a moment like that to myself. Rescuing Amos. Confronted with death and such. Did I have to do everything myself? Was there ever a right-Dao day gone wrong? I decided I may as well to get back to Ghost's and at least inform him that his community burgers had not been flipped. Or, cosmos help me, flip them myself— seize the spatula, reach into the darkness and hellish heat of the Weber grill, scrape up his apostles, turn them, dang them down to new flames. I needed to talk to Ghost, get his ear, didn't know what I'd say, only I wanted to know how he did doing nothing. He'd faced death so many times, shouldn't it have given him a little look behind the cosmic curtain?

Shortly after I pulled in, Amos, Trudy B, Wolf Man, and Ellie showed at Ghost's place, where the community burgers' mist had subsided. My shift was over. I was hungry, hungrier than I'd ever been.

We found the old hobo, spry as ever, mashing his groanbox to a new random verse.

When spring time comes, oh won't we have fun.
We'll throw off our jobs and go on the bum.
Hallelujah, I'm a bum!

I figured, after we all ate, I'd get him alone, let him sober up some, and talk.

Trudy B went into Ghost's house to get paper plates, forks, and such. She set them on the picnic table. Wolf Man's sister wheeled herself up to one end. Wolf Man sat next to her, examining a taxus-scratch, back of his left paw. Amos came up, sat down. I noticed how we were scattered at the table. After events of that day, I got his weird sense we were glad to be scattered, somehow felt safer that way.

All heads turned when we heard the *ying-ying-ying* of the crotch rocket, and saw, one block back of Ghost's, Fayteh's Cavalier in hot pursuit, in frame-shots between houses, pushing at least ninety, way past what the Cavalier was capable of.

Go, Fayteh Mann! I thought. Crack the horizon! Get that mother. Drag him back to Luckey, once and for all!

A little later, Ellie wheeled herself over to the Weber. Wolf Man followed. He lifted the lid and hung it on the rim.

"How's them burgers?" Amos said.

"Hallelujah, I'm a bum!" Ghost interjected.

"Yeah, you *The One*," Amos sniggered.

And that's when Wolf Man touched a single tine of a single fork to a single burger among the twelve gathered on the grates of Ghost's community grill—and the holy burger crumbled into dust.

"Ashes," Wolf Man said.

Trudy B came over, touched another burger, and it disintegrated at her fingertip. She shook her head slowly like it was her fault, then put her ashen finger to her tongue to taste it.

I was end-of-time hungry. I swear I tried to stop myself from crossing over to Ghost's chaise. But I swung around, stopped in front of Ghost, took him by his arms and silenced his groanbox.

"Our burgers are all ashes!" I said. "What world are you living in? Can't you see what's going on around here?"

"Yes, I can," he said.

Ghost rose a little from his chaise, so quickly I wondered if he'd been capable of such a feat all along. He gestured in the air between us for me to come closer.

"Well?"

I crouched to meet him there, that half-suspended old hobo, *The One*, maker of ashes.

"Truth," he said, "fuck off."

SURVIVAL HOUSE

I will show you fear in a handful of dust.

-T.S. Eliot, *The Wasteland*

The first time I saw my young wife Cassie with eighty-year old Mr. Quart, they were standing on the porch of Quart's little ranch she wanted to rent. They watched me through the picture window, each an index finger at their foreheads, a salute to cut the glare and get a good look at me, as if I were the solitary renter, and they landlord and landlady.

When Cassie and Quart snapped their sun-salutes off their foreheads, she left Quart on the porch and joined me inside the house.

"Just look at him," she said. "You wouldn't believe he's eighty years old."

"I believe it."

"But you wouldn't believe he was at eighty atomic bomb detonations in the 1950s, at the Nevada Test Site, and only has a touch of prostate cancer and hearing loss."

"I believe the hearing loss part," I said. "Did the old boy even hear our counter offer?"

"But this ranch is one of a kind," Cassie said. "It's the only survivor of the Survival Town test explosion in 1955. Well, not exactly a survivor. Mr. Quart says he was in charge of building suburban ranches so they could blow them up." Cassie looked fondly about the kitchen, the old 50s décor, wallpaper blurred with fleurs-de-lis, brown clay kitchen tiles, a bright white, Formica-clad kitchenette trimmed in chrome, a matching table with two tiny leaves tucked into one corner. "Quart stole the plans from the government," she added. "He built a house from Survival Town right here."

"So, we'll be living in something built for the sole purpose of being vaporized in an atomic blast."

"Exactly." She leaned into light slanting in the window, beamed, a dazzling corona erupting from her red hair. My love. My sun. She leaned in, kissed me. "This place is a remnant of BEEF, the Big Explosions Experiment Facility. I know it's scary to think about. But there's nothing to be afraid of. It'll be fun."

Out back, Cassie's Buster Beagle started howling his head off like an air raid siren. When the din diminished, I heard him bark, run the length of his chain, the stake snap him by his neck onto his side, eliciting a gush of air, a yelp, and more barking, culminating in another mad rush to free himself. Then the siren went off again.

On the porch, Quart'd again taken to the salute-look through the picture window. Cassie continued saying something about how interesting the old guy was. I looked back through the pane at his lips, colorless, undifferentiated from the pallid whiskerless skin surrounding them, fissured from eight decades of stress, sun, and gamma rays. To that, add Quart's entirely bald head, and the old man looked like one of the saucer-men that allegedly visited Earth in the 1950s. Roswell. Area 51. All that.

I went into the kitchen, opened and inspected the milk chute, obsolete in our time. Even in Ohio farmlands milk was no longer home-delivered. I knew Cassie was watching me play with the milk door. I wanted her to think I was curious about the place, a half-mile off the main road, end of a narrow dusty strip that divided six-hundred acres of soy beans in half and peppered the undercarriage of our car with stones. I wasn't really interested. But newly married, I tried to be.

"Anyway, it's done," Cassie said. "We're renting this place."

I turned to face my magnificent, frizzy, redheaded bride, reminiscent of Orphan Annie, alone from age six, when her father died suddenly of a stroke, abandoned by the woman Cassie called "some-professional-or-other person." Fourteen years later, Cassie still had this habit of writing letters to her dead father, said it helped her cope. Maybe she saw old Quart like a father and had gone soft in negotiating our rent.

"You're renting," I said.

My beautiful sun'd gotten her atoms excited over the prospect of renting a piece of apocalyptic history, her specialty studying in college, and I supposed part of her personal history, since she shared a birthday with Robert Oppenheimer. So I didn't stop her when she returned from the porch with the lease. We sat at the tiny white table and spread the document over a leaf. She signed the lease and handed to me.

Cassie counted, "Five, four, three, two . . ."
Buster Beagle was eerily silent out back.
"Very funny," I said and signed before she reached zero.

I told myself Cassie's and Quart's spying on me through the picture window was to see if I approved of Survival House. I didn't. I'd wanted a townhouse in Wapakoneta, circa 1925, cheap, but the green-gray slate roof leaked and furnace pilot extinguished every other try. The landlord assured Cassie they'd be fixed, his words met by one of Cassie's skeptical squints.

I was straight out of grad school, first job with an Ohio environmental consultancy, assigned nine months to study sustainability in the Ottawa River, as impaired by municipal and industrial discharges from Lima. Cassie and I'd been married the week before, just back from Las Vegas, what Cassie called 'Glitter Gulch.'

"Remember the 'Atomic-Powered' Elvis impersonator?" she said when we returned.

Now, back in Ohio, Elvis, the Ottawa River, marriage, maybe having kids, got me thinking about the sustainability of everything, the hope of our generation and those to come. But the only thing that felt sustained was my fear that someone may get reckless and ruin it for us all.

Cassie's degree in history got her a temporary job at the Neil Armstrong Air and Space Museum in Wapakoneta. She could have made more cashiering at Farmer Jacks but, as she put it, "Who knows what kind of greatness can sprout from these soy bean fields."

My first day of testing on the Ottawa River finished early, and I was happy to get home to Survival House. Results were not good, depressed levels of dissolved oxygen in the river. The black muck we dredged up from the bottom smelled sulfurous. Fish were suffocating. I hated knowing what would come next. In nine months, the report. Notice of probation. Appeal. Variance—another word for compromise. A consent order and ten-year plan to bring the maimed river around. Ten years. A win-win for the EPA and polluters, but not for the Ottawa.

When I pulled onto the half-mile gravel road leading to Survival House, I noticed again how oddly situated it was, isolated by soybeans both sides, under a wide blue sky. I used my time alone to get to know the place. I pulled up and found Buster Beagle out back, miraculously where we'd left him, staked to his chain. He'd worn himself out blasting away at the stake and lay pancaked in the shade of his doghouse. When I stopped to fill his bowl with fresh water, he raised one bloodshot eyelid, then let it fall back in a kind of blind aftermath of something awful. A shadow passed over me. I looked quickly enough to see a low-flying hawk headed for the southern bean field.

I went back inside through the patio door, into the kitchen, and noticed that the door of the milk chute was ajar. I got that prickly feeling you get when you feel threatened, like you're not alone. I prowled the house, first the bigger bedroom, a smell of fresh white latex, some splatted on the black baseboards, then went into the hall and smaller bedroom, blue, a different smell, almost oily, boy oily, a boy's room, perhaps someday. The bathroom was clean, bright, and toilet American Standard, what else. The kitchenette remained to be christened, ready for someone to get cooking. Nothing else seemed out of place, no one around.

After a time, I forgot about the milk chute. Survival House seemed so new, so unlived, ready for first occupants, Cassie and me. I supposed that made the outrageous rent Quart had extorted from my atom-admiring wife not so bad. But the feeling of the house was more than that, like the way the late-day Ohio sunlight illuminated living room drapes, not a reflected light, but one that seemed to radiate feebly from the fabric itself. It was a light one might imagine in last seconds of life when you're most alone. A frightening light. A personal light. A light meant for me.

When I got out front, I noticed how Quart had sodded the lot with perfect squares so green they seemed pure chlorophyll. But at its edges the lot terminated in dust and debris. Quart had left pieces of concrete-slathered two-by-fours, jagged, twisted strips of angle iron, gypsum mounds of rust-stained drywall, and all manner of nails. Nature struggled to reclaim the alien landscape. Where the lot met the southern bean field, a lone crabapple tree stood, dead, dry, witchy limbs on one half, the other half with buds waiting to bloom, a wonder since it was already June. Beneath the crabapple, a solitary dandelion stood, its flower half-cracked open. So much wreckage surrounded Quart's perfect plat of green that Survival House itself looked like it had been dropped from another planet to see if it could sustain life in spite of its hostile borders.

I wandered back to the porch, thinking how Adam must have felt in Eden, not seeing the picture of his entire world, when the shadow of a hawk hovered over me again, as if patrolling the limits of my paradise.

I heard Cassie's car coming on the gravel, then saw it stop about an eighth-mile out the drive. I parked myself in the nylon webbing of a lawn chair to watch her get out, then Quart get out, and both lean against her right quarter panel. They assumed their weird double-salute in the sunlight, shading their eyes, staring at me and Survival House. They stayed some time at that distance, until light softened in the sky, then got back in her car and drove off.

About fifteen minutes later Cassie returned, alone. She got on the porch and stood straight-up over me in my lawn chair.

"I want to have a baby," she said.

"All right," I said.

And she went inside.

A little later that night, various critters bleating in the bean fields about our atomic oasis, Cassie held forth over our tuna noodle helper and apple pie she'd made from scratch, our marriage pie, she called it.

"Not many guys like Mr. Quart are left from the old atmospheric days," she said.

"Atmospheric?"

"Device tests in open air."

"Device?"

"Atom bomb."

"Oh."

"When he talks about the Device, he has a cute way of saying 'tickling the dragon.' And you don't get guys so polite anymore, the way he says, 'with all due respect,' and 'I don't mean to criticize you people,' meaning people like you and me. But he's seen things. Mr. Quart says his first test they told him to turn away from the flash, and he did, but when he raised his hands to cover his eyes, he could see the bones in them, like an x-ray."

"Now, there's a party trick," I said. "Where's the old boy live, anyway?"

"Oh, sorry, he's sworn me to secrecy, says if I tell you someone from the CIA will come and terminate us both."

I dropped my fork in a small pile of apple filling.

"I'm kidding," she said.

But she hadn't said where Quart lived, and I didn't want to press the matter. I didn't need her thinking I was ridiculous, jealous of an eighty-year-old remnant of the Cold War.

"How's work at the Armstrong Museum?" I asked.

"Fine—oh, speaking of the Moon, Mr. Quart says they wanted to nuke the Moon back then. Project A119."

"What in hell for?"

"'Weapons in space' was all he said."

That night in bed with Cassie, I couldn't shake the feeling that Survival House was more mine than Cassie's, the way she explained everything to me, like I was being indoctrinated into its apocalyptic charms. I'd never wanted it in the first place, still didn't, but something made me think I belonged there.

When we started making love, I was focusing on a strawberry birthmark just above her left nipple, shaped like head of a toy poodle.

The little mark was part of our ritual.

I chanted low, "Poo-*dle*, poo-*dle*," part of our carnal cadence, concentrating on the mark, announcing my intention to climax.

Cassie hooked me at the neck and drew me close, said, steamy, breathy in my ear, "Don't you think it looks more like a mushroom cloud? Say, 'mush-room-cloud.'"

I stopped.

She stopped.

"I can't say 'mush-room-cloud.' It ruins the rhythm," I said. "You think it looks like a mushroom cloud?"

It did look like one.

"I want to have a baby," Cassie whispered.

I didn't want a baby.

"Okay by me," I said, burped out "mush-room-cloud," and resumed pushing, not arguing with my beautiful new wife at such a critical moment. But I began to get confused, humping and hissing "mush-*poo*, room-*dle*," my former two-syllable cadence, which elicited a vaginal spasm from Cassie—then stillness, the only sound the chirruping of insects in the bean fields, the way something can be so loud you can't image it ever ending.

I was an odd breakfaster, next morning reached into the fridge for a piece of cold leftover apple-pie, and found the whole thing gone. I prayed, not being a praying man, that Cassie'd taken our marriage pie to work, and not to Quart. I also noticed that one leaf of the kitchenette was raised, like someone had joined Cassie for breakfast. Had to be Quart. Quart again. Always Quart.

When I got to the Ottawa River, I remembered my team had the day off. I did, too. I smiled, thinking how automatically I was connected to my job, how much I wanted to get out of Survival House, away from Quart—and Cassie's obsessions with the man and Survival House. So I was glad I'd come to the Ottawa. I lingered there, watching the olivine water pimple and flow beneath a parade-line of low-hanging oak and willow. I guess I wanted the Ottawa to take me somewhere else, like Huck and Jim, anywhere. Then I spotted the roots of one willow, like a hand clutching the riverbank, hanging on, and soon my hands dug into mud at my sides. I had to stay. Had to. Quart or no Quart, what sort of man turned sour on his new wife? If that willow could hold on, so could I.

I drove home with a new resolve to stick it out in Survival House. I didn't want a baby, but I wanted Cassie, and so the math said I wanted a baby. Well, okay.

When I pulled up to the ranch, there was no mistaking the new addition to our little piece of history. Someone, obviously Quart, had erected a steel tower, around fifty feet high. Left side of the house. At first I was grateful. Our rabbit ears could barely pull in television stations from nearby Lima. And then I saw, even in the bright day, top of the tower, the tiny red light flashing on and off at two-second intervals. I was about to work out the puzzle of the red light when I heard—then saw—Cassie's car on the gravel drive. She stopped about a quarter-mile out from the ranch. She and Quart exited the car and again ceremoniously parked themselves on Cassie's quarter panel. I saw a couple flashes, realized each had a pair of binoculars, and together were spying on me. I'd had enough of their Cassie-and-Quart-in-Black surveillance of me, started for my car to drive out there, then she and the old guy got back into her car and drove the rest of the way in. When they pulled up, Cassie got out alone and left the engine running. Behind the tinted windshield of Cassie's car I could see Quart's craggy Moon-surface face and lips, his black shades, watching us.

Cassie joined me on the porch, stuck her hands to her hips, and looked up at the steel tower and red flashing light. Her red orphan hair jiggled in the breeze.

"How do you like it?" she said.

"TV, right?" I said.

"Well, sort of . . . Mr. Quart had it prefabbed and some guys came out this morning to set it up. It's a miniature replica of the tower that held the Apple-2 Device that vaporized Survival Town. It's one-tenth scale. One-*tenth*!"

"Great," I grunted.

"The Apple-2 mushroom was rainbow-colored," she went on, "shot into the sky so fast an icecap formed at the top. At the bottom, the intense heat melted sand into smooth glass. Melted aluminum straight off the studs. Blew Survival Town into piles of dust. Twenty-nine kilotons. Twenty-nine. I know it doesn't sound like much these days. But Mr. Quart says it was a great success in his day."

"Success?" I said.

"I mean, the Device can be a terrible thing, but with all due respect, dear husband, we can put all that power to peaceful uses. Mr. Quart says look at the Davis-Besse Nuclear Plant. Take Cedar Point. Do you know how much power it takes to run coasters like the Magnum XL-200 or the Millennium Force? And they could use the Device underground to blast out canals, like in Panama. All those possibilities had not the SALT talks put Mr. Quart out of a job."

When Cassie'd uttered "SALT" I swear I saw Quart's lower Moon-lip curl at the edges in a snarl.

"So, what's up with the red light?"

"It flashes to let them know the Device is all right, ready to go."

"It's okay by me if you want to play the old boy's little Survival House game," I said, a diversionary tactic to get to the heart of the matter. "But what about our marriage-fucking-pie!"

"I gave it to Mr. Quart. He's dying. I felt sorry for him. Now he says the prostate stuff has spread. That's why he's renting the place. To help with expenses. He's completely impotent now. Can't you at least let him have his little dying fantasy of atomic destruction? Can't you?"

I looked up at the blinking reminder of mass mortality.

"Come on," Cassie said. "Get in my car. You and I and Mr. Quart can go all the way out to the end of the drive. We can see what the whole set-up looks like. Trust me, it's cool. Quart's a funny guy. He knows you call him Old Boy. He calls you Little Boy, like the Device they dropped on Hiroshima."

"Hilarious," I said. "But no."

I went inside, sat at the kitchenette table awhile, worked its leaves in and out a couple times, remembered the oaks and willows and Ottawa River.

When I heard the front screen click and car door snug shut, I knew Cassie and Quart were gone.

I went out to check on Buster, again pancaked in the shade of his house, his stake secure. I thought about letting Buster Beagle go, just once, just to see how truly independent the little clown really was, just to prove the little brute a fake in all his yanking and pulling and barking to get free. I believed he needed us, Cassie and me, but would not admit it to himself. But thinking that made me feel even more staked to Survival House.

Passing the living room, I stopped, felt something'd been added, but couldn't decide what. Quart again? I had to figure it out, the way people place things in a room in memory to detect an intrusion. I sat on the Quart-furnished brown and yellow paisley couch, and made a mental image. Across the room, a bronze bonsai tree painted on a lampshade. To its left, another shade with a tiny arched wooden bridge. Where my feet rested, a purple vinyl hassock. All familiar. I looked straight across the room to the picture window. In its glass, I saw the faint reflection of me on the couch, and the reflection of my back in the mirror on the wall directly behind me, two separate sides of me at the same time, both vague, uncertain. I remembered solid objects in the room just fine. But among them, I felt I may not exist at all, except as a kind of thing in abstract, a creature of angles and distances.

When I could not bear looking at the ghost of me in the picture window, I looked at the wall, left of the window, a black-and-white photo of a young woman. She had not been there when we moved in. The words "Pricilla, 1957" were written in the bottom right of the photo. She had blond, finger-cut curls smoking out a dark pillbox hat. A veil shaped like an astronaut's bubble enshrouded her head, mesh so fine it seemed like an electron fog about a nucleus. Her face was cocked up, ego-angled, vogue. Her eyes were straight-on, the sort that penetrated the veil and haunted the whole room, like she owned it. But the oddest thing: she'd been photographed only as a dim reflection in a rain-splattered windowpane. It seemed she and I were both trapped, indistinct, reflections of ourselves, surviving alone behind our veils.

Sunday morning at breakfast, I watched Cassie's teeth shredding her Shredded Wheat. Impatient. As if breakfast was a kind of wall to gnaw through. Behind her, the hawk flew high against the sun, then swooped in, plucked a hapless rodent from the dirt, then soared back, heavenward.

I nodded at Cassie, past her shoulder.

"A survivor if I ever saw one," I said.

She twisted back far enough to make of show of being interested.

I snapped.

"I don't remember that photo in the living room. Did you hang it in there?"

"Priscilla," she said, dabbing milk from her chin with a paper towel. "Tested 1957, Frenchman Flats, 37 kilotons. Mr. Quart's dead wife."

"But how'd that photo get there?" I asked.

She set her paper towel down. I waited for a reply, until out back I heard a new and uncharacteristic clank, followed by a sustained clinking. I raced onto the porch. Buster had broken out. I saw him round the side of Survival House and race into the bean field straight into the dive-trajectory of the hungry bird. There was a sound, like a pronounced "phew!" and an explosion of feathers. When I arrived at the site of mayhem, Buster'd already ravaged the hawk, a blossom of bloody down at my feet and a trail of crushed soy plants where Buster'd headed out with his prize, predator become prey.

I knew I'd never see the beast again, that he'd at last set out on his own path of survival. I turned back to Survival House, its girded tower atop which I was to imagine Quart's Device awaited, its pulsing red light, a kind of slow heartbeat.

I thought for sure the Buster calamity had stirred Cassie to join me on the porch. It hadn't. I went inside to find her, to give her the news. I heard her rummaging in the second bedroom, and when I got here saw a foot ladder and the trap to the attic pushed aside. Cassie was scooching a plain, white Formica cradle to a spot by the small window that looked out back, while gently lowering a mannequin in the form of a baby into the cradle.

"A mannequin baby?" I said. "Really?"

She set the plastic child down before speaking.

"Cool, huh? Mr. Quart says to call it a big doll. Mannequin contains the word 'man' and something like sounds like 'kin,' like 'man-kin,' too human a name for a test object intended to be vaporized and subjected to unimaginable quantities of gamma radiation."

I was not going to let her divert the conversation to Quart's Cold War lingo. I was ready to blow my top.

"Has Quart been coming in here?" I blurted. "I mean, doing things?"

"Doing? Like what?" she replied, face slack with innocence.

I wanted to mention the open milk chute, the leaf propped up, Priscilla in the living room. But I knew I'd sound crazy.

"That's not what I mean," I said, gawking at the plastic infant in the crib. "What gives with this doll-baby-thing-whatever?"

"It's not just the baby," she said, and glanced at the attic. "Mom and Dad are up there, and there's a big brother and sister. Come on, help me get them down."

I shrugged, somehow defeated again. I went back to the living room and stood at the picture window. The sky was pale blue, crisscrossed by two jet vapor trails. Soybeans quivered in a tepid wind, lacerated by the crushed path left by Buster trailing off into infinity. Quart's steel tower flashed red, brooding over the half-open dandelion and wizened crabapple. I tried to find some trace of myself in these things outside Survival House, the way I had before with objects in the living room, but couldn't, even in abstraction.

Then I saw a flash of light, a full half-mile off, out at the main road, this time the speck of Quart by himself, leaning on his pickup with his damnable spyglasses.

I felt Cassie come up behind me. She ran her arms under my shirt, up my back, then slipped them under my arms in a hug.

I saw both our faces dimly reflected in the picture window, and both looking beyond it, both watching Quart in the distance, watching us.

This time, the rushing realization was hard to stop.

"All this baby crap," I said, still facing the strange man a half-mile off. "It's Quart's idea, isn't it?"

"He only wondered when we'd start a family."

Cassie's voice sounded strange coming from behind me.

"That's all?"

"And he thought it would be neat if we started it in Survival House."

"Why?" I asked. "What does he care!"

"I don't know," my fire-haired bride whispered, hot in my ear. "Come on, Little Boy. You spend too much time with that river. Let's make a baby. If it's a girl, Mr. Quart says we can name it after a daughter of uranium, Thorie, like Thorium. If it's a boy, Thor will do."

She took my hand, turned me, and led me into the big doll's room. We stood by the cradle. With one hand she rocked it, each oscillation a tick in time.

She reached into my pants and seized my cock.

Somehow, I sensed Quart in the room with us, watching, waiting.

"Won't be long now," she whispered.

She slid her pinkie under one ball, like a trigger finger.

"Five…four…three…two…"

I closed my eyes before she reached zero.

STORY OF A POSTCARD

The image of the Humpback Covered Bridge shivered on the postcard tucked in the visor of Hearne's car. When he glanced back to the road, the countdown began: county roads eight, seven, four, all squirreling through rises and valleys the way he imagined the *Pequod* must have through crests and troughs of waves in search of Ahab's nemesis. Though not a sperm whale per se, Hearne's Humpback was no less challenging. He'd purchased the postcard at a rummage sale east of Cleveland based solely on momentary intrigue, and set out with ebullient, expectant faith that such a mysterious thing could be found, a man flung into the wild and indifferent universe of southern Ohio, knowing only the spot where the wily Humpback crossed Raccoon Creek, a single landmark among a web of gravel and dirt arteries.

Hearne pressed the gas pedal, urged his new Mitsubishi Starlight Silver Mirage faster, tightened the steering wheel in his hands, and jacked himself a little from his seat to peer over the next rise. Any moment now and one, no two, maybe six, or seven more rises, and the Humpback would break the surface of the curvaceous Appalachian foothills.

Then there it was.

Something so jaw-dropping Hearne stomped on the brake.

The Mirage skidded sideways to a stop, tail coming around and dust boiling up in a whirlpool around him.

$5,000 REWARD
FOR THE ARSONIST
WHO BURNED THIS BRIDGE
JUNE 6, 2013

The bridge's road surface had collapsed in a charred path into Raccoon Creek, but because the Humpback's tin roof and tresses had been arched, they not had fallen along a straight line, resulting in a twisted spine that looked like the wrenched ribcage of an animal tortured before torched.

Above Hearne, poplars quaked, leaned over the scene like curious sleuths. Hearne felt his heart plunge into Raccoon Creek along with his slain Humpback.

He saw an old man sitting near one of the charred pilings, a rod and reel in his hands.

The old man waved Hearne over.

"What burned the Humpback," the man said, "was the ghost of the same miscreant buried beneath violets in the meadow below that burned the bridge here in 1874."

"That so," Hearne said.

"I know so," the man called after him. "Before the fire, I dreamt I saw him set it, dreamt I beat the flames with my jacket, and when I woke I had burn marks on my hands!"

The man turned his palms up to show scarlet blisters salved with something like butter.

When Hearne had told his coworkers at corporate that his first stop on vacation would be the Humpback, they looked at him askew, said:

"Poor fellow."

"Have fun."

"You really do need to get away from all this."

And he supposed he did. The short of it, shorter the better so he could get on with his life: married to a small-town Wapakoneta high school sweetheart and cheating wife. No-fault divorce. His very clever attorney preying profitably on his ex-wife's guilt, who insisted that she'd once loved Hearne madly on account of his quixotic nature, often leaving purplish-yellow hickeys on his neck she called his "Sancho Panzas."

But his impulsive nature was no longer charming.

"Quixotic?" he said. "Am not!"

"How would you know the reality of being quixotic," she replied, "if you're hopelessly quixotic?"

A week after the divorce, he got his first big job at corporate in Cleveland, straight out of Ohio University. He bought a singles condo, closet stocked with muted pinstriped suits, neckties his coworkers had to help him tie. He acquired a brief taste for art films at the Cedar Lee Theatre, where he found himself hating *The Tin Drum*, but always ready to play upon it to impress coworkers at social gatherings in the Flats.

He acquired an appetite for tequila straight, a kind of rite: the salt a preparation for life, the shot itself a libation that not only empowered, but wounded and betrayed, and the lemon that cleansed the bitter taste of everything away. All worked beautifully in concert, until one night when his inebrious state left him telling and retelling the story of his divorce to the point two coworkers had to help him to the Terminal Tower and onto the train headed to Strongsville, a few minutes after which he passed out, then woke, with the driver rousing him.

"We've gone clean out to Strongsville and back to the Terminal. You want to try for home again?"

Ergo, Hearne's boss's suggestion for a vacation, which he dutifully accepted, took a too-long meditative walk downtown, along the break wall of Lake Erie, not pondering his wife's betrayal, but a future, the success of which would forever separate him from her, her ilk, and small-town-anyone else.

He'd wanted to find the Humpback on the postcard.

On his own.

He wanted to win.

He didn't ever want to be betrayed again.

Hearne walked back to the Mirage, removed the postcard of the Humpback Bridge from the visor, folded and placed it in his wallet. As he drove north to Hocking Hills, the next leg of his vacation, he struggled to comprehend the Humpback's misfortune in terms of his personal misfortune. He felt foolish to have put so much trust in the postcard, like he'd trusted his ex-wife, an image, a bridge, a wife, whatever, that only brought to mind the thing it suggested, never the thing itself.

There were thirty-three campsites at the family primitive hike-in camp in Hocking Hills. His was number twenty-three, one of the farthest from the park office and parking lot, about a half-mile trek.

No one occupied the sites either side of his. He consulted the brochure the ranger'd given him. Fresh water all the way back at the office. Three pit latrines, equally spaced. He shook his head, caught himself mapping things, thinking about the postcard of the Humpback, how things may not be what they seem. He tore up the brochure, pledged himself to a new reality. He would only believe what he saw. He would be practical. Logical. When he returned from vacation, his coworkers at corporate would say, "A very down-to-earth kind of guy."

His new outlook seemed to clear up something that had troubled him for years. One night, shortly after he was married, he dreamt he woke with dozens of human bite marks all over his body. When he in fact woke, he found a real bite mark on his left shoulder, two tiny white indentations blossoming out his pink skin, faint, a pinch, not enough to have immediately awakened him from deep sleep, but there, nonetheless.

He rolled over to find his new wife staring into his eyes, hungrily.

"Did you just bite me?" he asked, and when she didn't answer, repeated, "Did you?"

The second part of his utterance seemed to leave her crestfallen. She brushed her fingertip over the mark on his shoulder, said, "No, I didn't," and closed her eyes.

He watched her sleep awhile, her perfectly sealed eyes, mouth set in a kind of line-smile that curved gently in direction of each ear, like the enigmatic, fixed expression of a porpoise. She seemed so completely innocent. How could she have lied about biting him?

In the two years they were married, she never admitted to biting him, though he must have asked a dozen times.

"Jesus," she said, "I don't remember! Maybe it is what it is. You dreamt of being bitten and your own dream bit you."

Now, he was sure.

The old man's dream had not predicted the Humpback's demise or his burned hands. Likely, he'd burned the bridge himself!

Hearne's dream had not created the bite mark on his shoulder. The bitch had bitten him and she knew it!

At dusk, he set up his tent, pumped the cook stove, and boiled some ramen noodles. Before turning in, he got his propane lantern going with a pop and hiss, then settled against a log, legs crossed, and opened his copy of the Arden *As You Like It* he'd gotten at the same rummage sale as the postcard of the Humpback, another facet of his self-improvement, having not read an iamb of Shakespeare.

He'd also purchased a ticket to see the play at nearby Ohio University the next evening, and wanted to see what he could make of the play before going.

By act 2, Hearne decided it was a nice little play. Despite hardships, the duke feels enfolded and nurtured by nature:

> *And this our life exempt from public haunt*
> *Finds tongues in trees, books in running brooks*
> *Sermons on stones and good in everything.*

He slapped his Arden closed without finishing the play. Nature sealed the deal. He retired to his tent thinking he could not go wrong being the ascetic recluse of the family primitive camp—at least for a week.

About three a.m. he slipped his sleeping bag past his knees, crawled out his tent, and regarded, quite by accident, the Big Dipper, cold and blazing above the horizon. He nearly wept. In nature, how could there be a more true connection than a solitary man and distant stars?

At sunrise, he felt a strange tingling on his lips. He smiled, thinking about his personal stars, then reached to his mouth to discover a huge red centipede stationed there, which he unceremoniously batted away and, with little sympathy for the nurturing aspects of nature, crushed the skittering creature with his Arden *As You Like It*.

"Crap!" he said, but was soon to discover the expletive no match for what he actually found later in the pit latrines.

He was thinking of leaving the campsite by the time he saw the family of six marching up the trail. They caravanned by past him, first the father, dark horn-rimmed glasses, an A's baseball cap, freckled, an expectant, relieved look on his face as he led his wife in her Capri pants, black-and-red striped pullover, her lower lip jutting out, rasping for air. Their brood followed, three boys stooped under large backpacks and a girl bringing up the rear, so tiny they'd not burdened her at all, and good thing since a fog of insects buzzed about her as she scratched and continuously swatted at the cloud.

Seeing them in such misery, floundering in his own, Hearne decided to stay at the Red Roof Inn in Jackson, a full forty miles southwest of Athens, a place he'd stayed before, and whose roof would likely be reassuringly red, unless it had burned down like the Humpback Bridge. He could catch the performance of *As You Like It* that evening, then head back to Cleveland. He'd secret himself at home a few days, then go back to work. For all any of his coworkers knew, he'd been primitive camping the whole time.

He hated to think it, but he took some comfort in the family's miseries. They seemed as lost as he was. The father set up a small stove on a pine stump, which chipmunks tirelessly investigated, kicking dirt and leaves at it. The boys revealed a badminton set, but soon found all three shuttlecocks stuck in thick canopies of trees. The mother strung a clothesline between two saplings only to have weight of wet jeans bend the young trees so far the clothes dragged in the dirt. When at last they erected their large tent, the small bug-bitten girl remained in the mosquito-netted canopy, alone.

The family seemed perfectly out of place, perfectly in tune with Hearne's newfound distrust of nature. He imagined the father stopping by and commiserating with him. They'd shake hands, swap a few stories, his about the ill-fated quest for the Humpback.

But it was the girl who broke out of her mosquito netting and ran in advance of her insect fog to his campsite first. She paused in front of Hearne a moment before the insects caught up with her.

"You here all by yourself?" she said, digging at her neck.

"Yes," Hearne replied.

He was ready to say he had some Off in his tent and did she want some. He was ready to find his new purpose as the happy-go-lucky, helpful single guy adopting a nice family as his own. He was ready to stay and combat the indifferent wilderness with them. But that was the whole of their exchange before the father raced over, retrieved his daughter, and placed her back inside the netting.

A little later, he saw the mother fry up some bacon and serve it between white slices of damp bread, all the while glancing suspiciously at Hearne. Then they packed up and caravanned out of the family primitive camp as orderly and methodically as they had arrived.

When Hearne woke the next morning, he lay in his tent a long time, brooding that the father and mother had thought he was some fearful skulking creature who preyed on children.

Later, he flopped the flap of his tent aside, crawled out, and stretched, surveying what he believed would be his very last look at primitive nature, not the duke's "good in everything." Rather, it was a miserable place of fear and mistrust, devoid of even simple human commiseration and company.

He was ready to head to his trusty Red Roof Inn, when he noticed a young man about his age pass, wave at him, and turn into the site abandoned by the family. After setting up his camp, the young man came straight over to Hearne and stuck out his hand.

"Hi, I'm Abe," the man said.

Hearne hesitantly took his hand.

"As in Abraham?"

"No, just the one word, Abe. It is what it is."

Abe seemed friendly enough to Hearne, 'enough' meaning he was in no mood to be taken in by his own imaginings of friendship, but after a time, talking with Abe, he noticed, beneath the man's red-and-black peppered moustache, the porpoise smile of his ex-wife's, which, even before her biting him, he had once deemed unchanging and genuine. The man proclaimed his love of hiking, and his calf muscles proved it. They seemed stone-cut compared to Hearne's stovepipes.

Abe spoke excitedly about hiking a few miles up to Old Man's Cave, like it was the most natural, easy thing to do.

"Why not?" Hearne said, and they set off.

Abe had been to Old Man's Cave many times, but it was Hearne's first trip into the deep, river-cut gorges, constant roar of falling water ever gouging deeper into rock, eddies forming large pools with sides striped tannic and gray. Some solitary pillars withstood the onslaught of water and time, while all else dissolved and rushed downward, ever down, a kind of cutting and wounding that never ceased, that created such painful beauty Hearne at last felt connected to something that was nothing but itself, no mirage of imagination, no betrayal of senses, something timeless and inexplicably itself.

Hearne was so overwhelmed he recalled *As You Like It*'s Jacques, standing "on the extremest verge of the swift brook anointing it with tears."

When they reached Old Man's Cave it was a large dark gash, canted downward into the side of a cliff, more than a cave, entrance cathedral-high, what Abe called the Shelter Cave, where, in the 1800s, the legendary 'Old Man' lived most of his life before accidently shooting himself using the butt of his rifle to break winter ice.

They stood by the cave's high stone walls for some time.

"Amazing," Hearne said.

"Amazing," Abe repeated, as if no other word could ever be used to describe the moment.

When they returned to their campsites, Hearne went to the showers to get ready to drive to Athens for the performance of *As You Like It*.

He was back at his site, toweling off his hair, when Abe stopped by.

"Where you off to?"

He told Abe he was off to Athens to see the play.

"I wouldn't have figured you for Shakespeare," Abe said.

Hearne put his towel aside and showed Abe his Arden copy of the play.

"I've read it," Hearne said. "It's pretty good."

Abe took the book from Hearne, examined it briefly, then returned it.

"Why don't you stay?" Abe said. "We'll get a fire going and swap our own stories."

"I have my ticket already," Hearne said.

"I'll buy your ticket," Abe said. "Please stay."

Hearne searched the man's eyes and face, finding only his ex-wife's porpoise smile, then went into his wallet, found the ticket tucked next to the folded postcard of the Humpback, and held it out to Abe as if doing so might erase the man's words, "Please stay."

"Stay—please," Abe repeated.

He waited for another word from Abe, some retraction, capitulation, anything. The silence was unbearable and, not getting a reply, Hearne ducked into his tent.

"I'm going," he said. "Leave me alone."

It was late, past midnight, when Hearne returned from Athens and the play.

Abe had broken camp and was gone.

In years that followed, that part of Hearne's past couldn't fade away fast enough. But when his coworkers at corporate asked about his trip, he told them the story of the burned Humpback Covered Bridge, the mysterious man who'd burned it, his primitive camping in Hocking Hills, but he always left out the young man he'd met there.

Years after that, when he met his ex-wife at his ten-year high school reunion in Wapakoneta, he was glad to see her. They had a couple drinks together, his tequila, hers merlot. They compared lives. She had a husband, two girls, was a graphic artist. He had not married, or changed jobs, but was promoted a couple times. He told her the story of the postcard and the burned Humpback Bridge. He still had the postcard, creased in half, where he kept it in his wallet. He removed it, flattened it, and set it, image-up, on the table between them.

"I just wanted one thing in my life to match up, to connect," he confessed. "You know?"

Then he told her of the Primitive Camp in Hocking Hills. This time he mentioned encountering Abe there, the young man's "Please stay," how the words haunted him, how for so long he'd wanted to know what the words meant.

"Words, words, words!" he said and looked for a reaction from her, only to see the unchanging countenance of the porpoise.

He shook a little salt in the crease of his thumb and forefinger, licked it, chased it with a shot of tequila, then crushed the bitter wedge of lemon in his teeth, making everything taste tart and clean again.

"Maybe Abe was gay," he said.

"Like that has anything to do with it," his ex-wife said. "Maybe you're a fucking idiot and that young man's words meant he liked you, and he was lonely. Plain and simple."

"I don't know," he said and couldn't think of a reason the young man should like him. "Why should he like me?" he added. "He didn't know anything about me."

She put a thumbnail to the edge of the postcard and nudged it his way.

"You didn't know anything about the Humpback." She lowered her voice the way people do to say something important. "And yet you went looking for it. Why can't you just accept the man liked you, Hearne? That he was lonely and may have just needed companionship?"

"You really think so?"

She reached over, turned the postcard of the Humpback Bridge facedown, then rose, leaned across the table, and bit him firmly on the shoulder.

"I know so," she said.

CHERRY PIE

The cashier at Winky's Café set my slice of cherry pie on the green tray of two boys in line behind me. I didn't say anything about the mistake. One boy was around twelve, the other six or so. Brothers, I guessed. I'd seen them counting nickels, dimes, pennies before getting in line, to see if they had enough to pay, and when they paid the red mound of crust and glittering sugar crystals mysteriously appeared on their tray. My slice of pie. Expensive pie. Pie for which I'd waited all day. The boys' eyes went wide. The little one nudged the big one with his forearm.

"Look at that," I heard him whisper.

"Shut up," the big one said.

The little one's mouth turned down, then his eyes, first to the time-worn image of a trombone on his tee shirt and words, "Glenn Miller Orchestra," then his pair of ratty gray Nikes. The big one had identically ravaged Nikes, jeans so taut and short they fully exposed his gray soiled socks. A large Salem Cigarettes tee hung to his knees. He kept taking a bolt of the Salem tee and nervously stuffing it in then pulling it out the waistband of his jeans. I recalled his tee had come free with a carton of Salems over twenty years before, times you could wear a shirt like that and not look ridiculous. Both tees made the boys look older.

Part of me hoped the two boys would get away with that illicit piece of pie, I suppose the same part of me that wanted to get away with being at Winky's in the first place. My wife had forbidden me to patronize the parlor of bad-for-you, steeping-in-a-filthy-metal-pan-for-hours food.

The cashier set my Philadelphia steak sandwich on my tray. She turned a little back to the kitchen, swung forward to face me again, then lifted the cherry pie off the boys' tray, their eyes all the while following the pie's trajectory, and expertly landed it on my tray.

I went to the self-service soda fountain, dropped a few machine cubes into my cup, pressed the cup against the fountain switch, and waited while the gush of dark liquid filled it, blinking from the glare of overhead fluorescents off the white tiles of Winky's. I closed my eyes and the gushing sound of soda gave over to a kind of ringing in my ears. When I opened my eyes, light seemed even stronger than before, so I focused on watching the two boys back in line, two miniscule, unadorned pale-gray burgers on their green tray. When the fountain gushing ended, just as the boys were turning away from the line to find a table, I went up to them. I say I went up to them not because I'd thought about it first; I swear I went mesmerized by the flow of dark liquid, the bright light, the ringing, the horrific sight of their blanched burgers.

"That piece of pie," I said to the big one and reached for my wallet; his eyes shot wide, something at the moment I took for surprise. "I'll buy you one."

When the little one smiled, eager-eyed, I felt justified in breaking my promise to my wife about not going to Winky's. I was meant to go to Winky's, meant to meet these boys and offer them a piece of pie. One generation in communion with another. A helping hand. All that. Winky's had the best cherry pie in town.

But the big one's mouth trembled, eyes narrowed.

"No, mister," he said, turned, and hustled the little one to a table the far side of the restaurant.

My wallet went back into my pants, a first reaction to the big one's display of primal fear.

I sat, my side of Winky's, and ate quickly, wounded by a rushing realization. The big one thought I was the stranger kids were not supposed to talk to, let alone accept a piece of cherry pie from. I was the lurking despicable thing that spirited children away from worlds of safety to those of unmentionable horrors. When I was a kid, there were mornings when you could hit your back door running and not be expected to return until dusk, times a kid didn't have to worry so much, times when I'd have accepted a stranger's offer for such a glorious slice of cherry pie. But now, even poverty, desire, the sweetest, tallest, most enticing hunk of pie could not overcome such dread.

When I got up to leave fear still lingered in the big one's face like a reflection of me, the monster in the mirror. I dropped my trash into the chute, got in my car, and powered on my cell. I had to talk to someone about that slice of pie, even if it meant I'd be busted. I called my wife.

"A funny thing happened at Winky's," I said.

"What were you doing at Winky's!"

"I know. I'm weak. Pathetic," I confessed. "But there was this funny thing—I tried to buy a couple poor kids a piece of cherry pie. But one of them got scared, like I was the boogeyman or something."

"It's not funny. Suppose he tells someone."

"Never mind," I said. "I'm on my way home."

I pulled out of Winky's, onto Liberty Hi, and watched the countryside go by. Here and there a lonely farmhouse stood, sharply outlined against the afternoon light. Long rows of mid-summer cornstalks stabbed at the skyline, soil at their root ends hot, red. Shadows of dense cornrows cut the road. I was grateful for the drive home, the way you drive, try to take in other things, try to put things like the big one's frightened look out of your mind, think if you don't you'll crash your car into those rows of corn.

I caught the steering wheel and held it fast at ten and two. I thought back to Winky's. What if my wife was right? What if the big one said something to his parents? What if he told them this old guy wanted to buy them a piece of cherry pie? Even if the big one meant it differently, not sinisterly, like he thought I may have been a good man, his parents may take his telling them about me as a slight on their parenting, like they were no good because it took a stranger to buy their boys a piece of cherry pie. Then the parents would start thinking the worst of me—me!—a stranger they could not possibly know, my only crime an odd concoction of condescension and empathy for their boys. I would be falsely accused, hounded by police, questioned, held to ridicule, photographed, good name spread ignominiously across the Internet. More distressing was the outside chance that the two boys might actually *be* abducted by a genuine bad man. Witnesses would come forward, say I offered to buy the two victims a piece of cherry pie. Witnesses. The cashier! What had possessed me to be so stupid, so unthinking?

I reached for my cell, figured if I called my wife I could establish I was on the phone with her at a certain time and location, and not up to no good. I'd seen on television that they can triangulate your location by pinging off cell towers. Something like that. I punched in her number, then realized it would not be enough to merely call her. She might suspect I called only to cover up something else. Besides,

I'd just called her a few minutes before. I started to power off my cell.

But she picked up.

"I'll see you soon," I muttered. "I'm about eight miles out on Liberty Hi. Just passed Poe Road. I left Winky's about eleven minutes ago."

"Whatever," she said and hung up.

I breathed a couple times, the way you make yourself breathe when you think something awful might happen, the sort of thought that'll run you clean off the road if you're not careful. I caught myself drifting to the berm, gripped the wheel tighter. I had to stop thinking and do something, and so turned into a short road accessing a cornfield, stopped near the darker reaches of the stalks. From my car I looked into the shadows of the corn row. Part of me wanted to get out of my car, press on through the stalks, come out the other side of the field, a place where Winky's, the boys, that piece of cherry pie never existed, where I'd be headed home into a big red sunset.

I'd only called my wife a second time to establish where I was and when. Dumb. Who was to say I hadn't snatched the two boys and had them in the car with me when I called her? I reasoned my innocence may depend on whether the cashier—mind, the cashier!—could remember me and the two boys together, and my offering to buy the piece of pie, so I backed out the access road, and headed off to Winky's again.

I was worried about what the cashier would remember, but it felt good to be back on the road. Dusk was coming on. Sounds of the countryside blubbered faintly at my car window, my cheek. For a few minutes I thought nothing of where I was headed, or why, just the direction, a peaceful momentum. When I pulled into the parking lot of Winky's the sun was getting low and the whole place flooded with a pale white light. Overhead, two purplish streetlamps buzzed. I entered the restaurant and spotted the woman who'd cashed me and the two boys out. She looked tired and I thought that's all the better since tired people probably didn't give a shit and told the truth, like when you're drunk or high. I studied her—young, thin, even bony, with sandy hair that ran out her cramped hairnet in misty strands, like split waterfalls you see in exotic places on *National Geographic.*

I waited in line a long time while the cashier shuttled food from kitchen to counter and ran the register. When I reached her, I asked only for a cup of black coffee. She seemed relieved for the easy ring-up.

"Do you remember me?" I said.

She looked me over while lowering the coffee cup to my tray.

"Should I?"

"I was in here about a half hour ago. I had the Philadelphia steak sandwich and a piece of cherry pie."

"No, don't recall," she said and dropped change into my palm.

"Are you sure? There were a couple boys behind me in line. You put my pie on their tray by mistake."

"No, mister," she muttered and glanced at the considerable line forming behind me.

I sat to drink my coffee and watched her carefully. When the line ended I watched her a little more, expecting her to come to my table and say she remembered me, the two boys, the cherry pie. But she put her backside to the counter, knobby spine to me. I heard her cough, exhausted.

I left Winky's relieved that the cashier had not remembered me. I got back onto Liberty Hi, realized I'd be home even later than I promised my wife, reached for my cell to seek forgiveness. But what would I tell her I'd been doing? Interrogating the cashier at Winky's? How could I possibly explain? So I left the restaurant and headed for the old 1970s strip shopping mall nearby, parked, and went into Odd Lots. I'd no plan going in there, and for a while became one of the wandering people who snags this or that from a shelf, smiles or jeers at the exotically eccentric, out-of-production oddity, and sets the thing back. Once I found a large rubber eyeball; you squeeze it in your fist and the red iris swells and shrinks in unimaginable ways, ways that make you wonder what it might be like to have such an eye, the way things might look, changing and misshapen, one moment to the next.

I phoned my wife.

"I'm at Odd Lots," I said, "somewhere between resin garden fountains with expressionless cherubs and Chinese imported adult diapers called 'Heavenly Absorbance.'"

"So?"

"I'm going to be a little later than I thought, that's all."

"Just come home, mister."

"Oh, wait, here's rainbow-colored duct tape from the Ukraine. Each strip is red, yellow, and blue. Didn't you want duct tape to patch up the cold air return for the furnace?"

After some silence, my wife said, "Okay," made a nasal sound, hissing, like air going out of a tire, and added, "just get it and get home."

What a deal. A nice fat roll of rainbow duct tape. A dollar—cheap, considering it had also furnished me with an excuse for my lateness.

Night had come full-on when I again passed Winky's, a little island of light in the darkness, dead inside, except for the cashier, hands and elbows resting behind her on the cash register, as though someone had propped her there and forgotten her. I felt bad for her, but glad she'd been so busy she couldn't remember me and the boys. But surely she'd go home eventually, rest up, and I had to think that people, just so refreshed, might remember things they had forgotten while tired. The cashier might recall me and the two boys, after all. Perhaps! How could she not eventually recall a big kid with a Salem tee, a little one sporting a trombone, and, especially, me, foolishly showing up to ask if she remembered the three of us and my offering that piece of pie? I slowed the car, found myself once again pulling onto an access road concealed between cornstalks, now dark, greenish walls of dread. The cornstalks stood against the moonlit sky, witchy and waiting—always waiting, perhaps concealing corn witches themselves concocting the most miasmic stew imaginable, forever murmuring their endless list of ingredients as they tossed them into their hot, bubbling cauldron of worry. But what was I really afraid of? The important thing was to assure myself that the two boys were alright. Even if they mentioned to their parents how I'd tried to buy them that piece of pie, it could not be worse than, say, that one chance in millions some authentic psycho actually abducted the two boys, or that, when they'd come into Winky's, they were running away from home. Either way, I could wind up getting blamed!

The boys had obviously walked to Winky's and so had to live in the vicinity, likely the rather old and shabby Gypsy Lane Trailer Park near Winky's. I backed out the access road and headed for Gypsy Lane, reasoning there was still enough light that I may spot the two boys walking around. But before I got to Gypsy Lane, I had one of my most brilliant ideas ever. Wasn't human communication the key to solving the world's problems? Wouldn't our strange race be better off if we were just frank and upfront about things? So I pulled into Winky's once more. My plan was to buy another piece of cherry pie, this time to-go, and if, just if, I were lucky enough to spot the boys playing around their trailer, I'd go straight up to their front door, pie in hand in its little Styrofoam wedge, knock, and ask to speak to their parents about the piece of pie, how I meant no harm, how I just really, really wanted them to have that piece of pie.

It seemed like a great thing to do. Who isn't more at ease when things thought of in the dark are brought out and seen face-to-face in the light of day? Only my newest dilemma had to do with the cashier. Again! If she did not recall my interaction with the boys before, when I went inside to order a second slice of pie, she may then. And if I could not find the boys or their parents, I was back to the beginning of my maze of worries. I reached into the backseat of my car, found a sweatshirt, and pulled it over my tee. Then, with my fingers, I combed my hair forward, partially covering my eyes. Satisfied with my disguise, I went in and purchased the slice of pie, the whole while the cashier watching the clock above the counter, counting minutes to closing, so intently I was sure to get away with my ruse, but when I headed out with my pie, she called after me.

"Sorry, mister," she laughed a little. "I still don't remember you and those two boys."

I was stunned by her brazen innuendo, so much so that I felt an even greater urgency that I find the boys' parents and get that piece of pie to them.

When I reached Gypsy Lane, I slowly, methodically drove the streets, passed poles with power meters nailed to them willy-nilly like strange totems, old silvery streamlined trailers with red fluted skirts, and one job with an odd slanting snout and windows mere slits above a longer picture window, the whole of which seemed the eyes, mouth, and countenance of the noseless Sphinx. I slowed, hoping for the Sphinx's riddle, for I knew the answer—me, a man, in all aching stages of life!—but she was silent.

When I found no sign of the boys, I parked a little while. It was a longshot, but maybe, just maybe I would catch a glimpse of one of the boys through a window. Or spot one chasing fireflies, which were by that time luminous, winking soft yellow in the night, so many, on and off, I started thinking that each wink of light was only one of a million bad things that can happen to a kid, and a million more that can happen to anyone. And it all starts when a cashier at Winky's sets a piece of cherry pie on a couple kids' green tray. A piece meant for you. You get scared, scared all the time, not of what you know might happen, but of what you can't know that will happen, until it happens, and the thought chokes the breath from you, until you lose your voice and there's nothing left but other people's questions and suspicions. I had to set this right. I had to!

Then, there he was, the little one who'd wanted that pie so badly, running out of his trailer. He cast his arm in the air with the sweep of a great net, caught a firefly in his fist, then went to his knees and smeared the efflorescent bug's thorax on the pavement, where it left a little glowing smudge. I heard his mom call him inside. He leapt up and dashed inside the trailer.

I took up the piece of pie, went straight to the door, and knocked.

A woman, the mother I assumed, came to the door. She looked a lot like the cashier at Winky's, tired, but older. Her teeth were edged brown. Coffee, cigarettes, or both. I could see the big one standing a few feet behind her.

"Excuse me," I said to the woman, "but earlier today I offered to buy your boys a piece of pie over at Winky's. I'm afraid I may have frightened the big one. But I really meant no harm. They seem like good boys. They know to not speak with strangers. That's great. But I wanted them to have this pie, so would you take it and give it to them? Honest, Winky's makes the best cherry pie in town."

The big one pulled the door open a little more, until he and the woman were both backlit by a television program that had some amateur singer belting out a song derived from a familiar oldie, scripted just for the show. It sounded like Sinatra, *I've Got You Under my Skin.*

Then I heard the same slow expulsion of air I was used to getting from my wife.

"Look, mister," the woman said, glancing back into the trailer, then intensely at me. "You get off my fucking doorstep now or I'm calling the cops."

I trotted away, got back into my car, and set the pie next to the Odd Lots bag containing the roll of rainbow duct tape. I tried to assure myself I'd tried my best to clarify the matter of the pie. Perhaps it was enough. But the mother's remark only confirmed my misgivings—offering that piece of pie to those boys was monumentally dunderheaded! I'd had it. I was finished. I called my wife to check in.

"Sorry, I'm running a little behind," I said. "I just went back to Winky's to get another piece of that cherry pie. I mean, for you."

"For me, my ass!" she said. "What are you up to?"

"Nothing," I said, then could not help but add, "do you think I'm scary?"

"What?"

"I mean you probably didn't think I was scary when we were married. I'm talking about now. Is there some change in me that makes me scary? Grotesque gray hair? My frightful paunch? That spine-tingling sour look you say I sometimes have when really I'm not thinking one sour thing, when, in fact, I'm not thinking anything at all."

CHERRY PIE

"Mister," she replied, "the day I'm afraid of you is the day you bury me."

I had to think about what my wife said. She liked to zing me with such mind benders. But before I could reply she clicked off, and I sensed flashing lights behind me, something I first thought were some emotional exaggeration of firefly light.

But it was a police officer. He tapped my window. I ran it down and he leaned in. I saw his gaze fall on the Styrofoam pie container on the passenger's seat, then to the Odd Lots bag containing my rainbow duct tape. Too dumb for words! What if he discovered I'd been talking to the two boys and had rainbow duct tape in my car?

"I have a report that you've been driving this neighborhood awhile," the officer said. "What's up?"

"Fireflies," I said and watched his eyebrows arch. "I mean I was slowing up to admire them."

The officer bent back a little to see the fireflies, then leaned in my window again.

"License and registration," he insisted, then took both back to his cruiser.

I was sure he was running my numbers, to see if I was in the system, see if I was a good man or bad man. I thought, what if there were some kind of bug in the system, like a typo, and you flash onto his cruiser screen like some psycho predator they're after, so they arrest you, then they trace you back, back to Winky's and that moment you reached for your wallet and offered to buy the boys a piece of cherry pie, and after that tried to get their mom to take another hapless slice, and they go back even farther, how far you can't know, and find something else, some awful thing in your past, especially since they think you're a psycho predator, and you're tried, convicted, moved secretly to a special prison, all alone, since you are so psycho and despicable that other prisoners will kill you, then, then, maybe after twenty years of this they catch their mistake and let you go, made into a doddering old psycho all because they thought you were a psycho.

The officer handed my license and registration back to me.

"Go home to Janie," he said.

"You know my wife?"

"We know everything, pal. She's in the system. You're in the system. Everyone's in the system. Just go home, okay?"

"Alright," I said, immeasurably relieved, so much so I blundered into saying, "would you like a piece of cherry pie, officer? I got it from

Winky's but my wife doesn't want it. Best pie around."

"No, mister," he mumbled, turned briefly to regard the fireflies winking on and off, and shook his head.

The officer followed me until I pulled onto Liberty Hi, heading home. A short while later, I again thrust my car into the cornfield and stopped. But this time I was no longer afraid of corn witches. Or police. Or the rustling rumors of cornstalks in the late night wind. The boys were alright. It wasn't any of that. I swear it was a firefly that sent me back into the dark field, one of the damnable creatures glowing my side of the windshield, defying my attempts to swish it out my car window. What good is light when it flashes on and off like that? What good other than to warn against something unimaginable, unspeakable? After a while, I gave up trying to expel the firefly. I set the second piece of cherry pie in my lap. I opened the lid. I ate the pie in my car, firefly light flashing on and off. I ate, red-handed, red–mouthed. I ate because awful things that might have happened never did. I ate because things that never happened still might. I ate mechanically, like a man undertakes a useless occupation. I ate until I was sugar-headed, tired, and ready to try for home again.

THE WORLD IS ENDING
YESTERDAY

He'll *not* rise straight from sleep, lingers half-awake, around him tranquility and disputatious voices entangled, believes sleep can obliterate certainty. He is *not* on a microbus headed for the Plokštinė Forest, *not* sitting next to Oscar, the world's most annoying young man. In his half-dream it is *not* now two-thirty p.m. and he is *not* on his way to a Soviet Inter-Continental Ballistic Missile site. In his daze, he is *not* one of the first Americans to tour the decommissioned site, and there have *not* been lethal levels of radiation only a few years before. In his slumber entwined in beautiful probabilities Oscar is *not* yanking on his arm, nagging, "Up you go, old boy. We're almost there!" followed by wind through the window of the microbus, pushing the tiny curtain into the interior, wrapping it about his head. It smells of wet ashes, a shroud for the dead. Through its muslin fog he sees Oscar's thin face, his shadowy features, like Mount Rushmore's Lincoln in slant, diffuse light.

"Mary and Joseph," he groans and glares at Oscar's visage.

"Sorry, Yank," Oscar croons.

"Stop calling me Yank," he curses—and curses himself for running into the only other American gracing the lodgings of the Hotel 'Crater' of Mažeikiai, the lodging's name a product of priceless atomic-age Lithuanian humor.

He takes a small bolt of curtain, wraps it over his eyes, and drifts off again, a deliciously drowsy state in which he does *not* share his American citizenship with Oscar, something Oscar mistakes as a right to rouse him at two p.m. in the afternoon to partake of the "ekskursija!" as Oscar put it in his overstressed, bad Lithuanian. Once more in a sleepy half-state he feels like an electron zooming toward a phosphorescent screen, uncertain of his location or speed until, smack up against the screen, he must yield his bit of light and reveal both.

Poor electron!

When he opens his eyes, he finds Oscar close, gawking at a point between and slightly above his eyebrows, as if boring into his skull.

"Sorry to stare," Oscar says.

"No you're not," he replies, flings the window sheer off his face, and regards Oscar in return, a man in his thirties, about the same age his father was when he died, a slim man, stick of wheat with rye-colored slacks and a blinding white shirt. A white plastic pencil holder nuzzles in Oscar's breast pocket, errant graphite scratchings adorning the top edge, reminiscent of cuneiform. Oscar takes a mechanical pencil in hand, twists the lead in, out. "That little scar," Oscar says and points the minuscule cylindrical tip of the mechanical pencil at the pock mark in his forehead. "Just there." He begins to recoil from Oscar's graphite-tipped thrust, and then relaxes. If nothing else, Oscar's accurate, precise, the way his father used to pride himself on freehand-drawing lines and circles.

He remembers sitting down opposite his father at the supper table.

Now observe, his father commands.

He watches his father tap two dots on the page, the slender barrel of the pencil snug against his thumb, his hand drifting above the surface. Its shadow glides above the page like a crow over new snow, several passes, descending imperceptibly with each pass until a faint gray line appears, a single stroke, and seems perfectly straight, dot to dot. All he can think: all the drifting, all the mystery involved in producing one pale line coming out of nowhere. And for what? To connect two faint dots? What pale theorem lies behind it? What science?

Oscar leans a little closer. "How'd you get that little mark on your forehead?" he says. "Why," he squints sourly and taps the end of his mechanical pencil on his thigh, "it's shaped a little like a capital 'G.'"

"I didn't know that," he tells Oscar and runs his tongue between his lips, like a blade through the seal of an old, undelivered letter. The microbus passes through an open area in the forest. He digs a little crystal of sleep out of one eye. Light pours in. He coils himself against the hull of the microbus and closes his eyes again. When the microbus stops rolling, he uncoils, gets out, and follows Oscar to one of four, ten-meter diameter asphalt domes rising above tall grass in a field ringed with pine trees. In the direction of Mažeikiai the pines curve east to a small lap of land formed by low hills, where he swears he hears a brook cutting through the peat floor of the forest.

THE WORLD IS ENDING YESTERDAY

The domes in the clearing are positioned at the corners of an imaginary square. At the center of the domes sits a fifth dome, "Like a center dot on the five-side of a die," Oscar says with a mixture of know-all and wonder in his voice. At the base of the central structure is an entrance to a rust-streaked concrete bunker leading underground. Oscar scrambles up the side of the dome, working his hands and legs like a crab. When he reaches the summit, he stands at attention. "Take one of me here!" he shouts, then moves a few paces, "No—here!" and a few paces more, "Okay, right here!"

"I don't have my camera," he replies, blinking, turning to head back to the microbus for a bit more sleep. "By the way," he pauses in his retreat, turns momentarily, "I wouldn't stand there long. Under the asphalt that thing is made of glass, like a large convex lens. You're likely to crash through."

"Ouch," Oscar says and comes spryly off the dome. "Say, how do you know these domes are made of glass?"

"My father was a rocket scientist," he says.

"Go on, Yank," Oscar grunts.

"He worked for NASA."

"No kidding," Oscar says and runs to his side. He wants to shout 'Heel!' but Oscar goes on, "Gee, I wonder what that was like, I mean, growing up with a rocket scientist for a father."

"It wasn't like anything," he says.

Oscar looks puzzled, then starts staring at his forehead again. He stares back at Oscar squarely, in imitation.

"Well, what's he like, your father."

He imagines his father standing outside the door of their apartment, not 'working' his key in the lock, but 'docking' it into the mechanism. Like Oscar, his father is tall. He's cloaked in a long, black overcoat, and the high white collar of his shirt pokes out the top. Only a sliver of his silver necktie shows. The rest runs into the dark depths of the overcoat, like his NASA secrets, his work enshrouded, "something to do with" the Apollo Project.

He only finds out after declassification that his father designed miniature nuclear reactors to power spaceships for missions beyond the Moon.

"My father isn't like anything," he tells Oscar. "He's dead."

Before he can sneak back into the microbus, the guide calls them all together at the entrance to the bunker, speaking first in Lithuanian and then English.

"Each of the four missile silos is connected to this central launch bunker," the guide begins.

"What," Oscar whispers, "connect the dots—liftoff, and blooey?"

The guide goes on to explain that the Soviet ICBM site was built in 1962 and dismantled in 1978 under SALT. Someone, not the guide, says the Lithuanians have been taking people through the missile site to annoy the Russians. Oscar's in an excited state, oscillating back, forth, bobbing up and down on his toes to see over the head of a tall Lithuanian woman topped with a beehive hairdo. He finishes by springing resolutely onto his toes.

"Hey!" he shouts to the guide. "Where'd they aim these things at, anyway?"

"Anywhere in the West," the guide replies. "When these missiles were decommissioned in 1978 they were intended for Cleveland," she adds, "U.S.A."

Oscar turns to him. "Did you hear that, Yank?" he says. "'Intended for Cleveland,' she says. 'Intended.'" Oscar shakes his head. "How about that? I thought that key-keeper fellow at the main desk of the Crater told me you were from Cleveland. Aren't you from Cleveland?"

He feels his mouth drop open, half-wide to answer Oscar's question (he is from Cleveland) and half-wide with incredulity that Oscar can publicly ramble so.

"Don't call me—"

"I know. Yank." Oscar vee-smiles. "Anyway," he adds, "all the time thinking about total annihilation. I don't know how people got through those Cold War days."

"I did," he says.

"Well, yeah," Oscar says. "But it's a new millennium. The world's different now, closer, more connected, don't you think?"

Strange. The young American talking machine wants to know what he thinks. Or is it purely rhetorical? He can't get the mystery out of his head, can't respond, and then notices how the tops of pines stand rigidly against the anemic blue sky, sharp, statuesque. From where he stands on the concrete stairs leading into the bunker, stiff high grass sawtooths everything he sees, as if not one molecule of any substance in air will stir for fear of raking against its terrible blades.

When they descend the cement stairs through a yellow-painted door, he notices a sign in red letters.

ВЫТРИ НОГИ

THE WORLD IS ENDING YESTERDAY

WIPE YOUR FEET

"Now the Cold War's over," Oscar says, "it's the least we can do." He smiles, scuffs the soles of his shoes on the spine of a rusted I-beam on the floor, and waits for him to do the same. They descend farther, into darkness, where overhead rusty water seethes, atomizes, and drizzles down from cracks in great gray slabs of concrete forming the ceiling and walls. At the bottom of the stairs, a feeble yellow light struggles to illuminate the corridor, emanating from infrequently strung helium lamps fastened to the right wall with bailing wire, all powered, someone in the group whispers, by a small village nearby.

They pass another sign.

ВОЗЬМИ ЖЕТОН
TAKE A TOKEN

"Token what?" Oscar laughs. "Token bombs?"

Another sign is nailed above it, but the Russian words are scratched out.

WAIT HERE THREE MINUTES—PREPARE YOUR EYES.

Waiting seems an eternity for Oscar. He fidgets, paces, then goes over to the cement wall and begins inspecting it for imperfections. "What're you doing here in Lithuania?" Oscar asks him, his voice sounding distracted by a divot of cement he's lifted from a long crack running curiously like the Mississippi River, its long variegated delta splaying the wall near the floor.

"Traveling," he replies, his eyes back on Oscar, who kneels and removes another chunk of Mississippi delta with his forefinger.

"Well," Oscar says, "I'm at the Mažeikiai oil refinery." He tosses the chip of cement aside and stands. "I'm a catalyst regeneration specialist."

"Regeneration," he mumbles because he believes if he mumbles something, anything, Oscar will not ask another question.

Again underway, they enter a long, narrow room. On its walls are ghostly outlines of long-gone control equipment. "To launch the missiles," the guide explains. From there they go down another dismal flight of stairs, toward one of the missile silos, past another sign, scarcely visible in the choked-out light, TAKE ANOTHER TOKEN, then up, along a small incline leading to a small circular room with the silo concentrically located. Metal grating that once connected the room to the silo is rusted through, or missing. Now a narrow wooden plank connects the outer room to a tiny trapdoor in the access hatch to the silo.

Soon others on the excursion fall to their hands and knees and creep along the plank toward the trapdoor, into the missile silo.

"You go ahead," he tells Oscar.

"Aw, come on, Yank," Oscar groans, impatient, watching the others disappear one by one through the trapdoor. "You heard our guide. There isn't any radioactive stuff left. They had real German scientists certify this place 'clean.'"

"Scientists," he mutters and tries to cover a yawn with his hand. "Real. German. Scientists."

Oscar pleads, "This could be your last chance to see one of these Cold War relics."

He doesn't respond, and after Oscar's derrière disappears into the silo, he's alone. Beyond the partly open trapdoor he hears the guide's muffled explanations in fragments, "six-hour shifts," "built in complete secrecy," "first thieves to ransack it died horribly of radiation poisoning." Listeners gasp, drop small stones off the railing, and wait for their eerie, echoic sounds plinking thirty meters below into ancient rainwater that has leaked through the glass dome overhead and collected at the bottom. He can see inside the open trapdoor, where the others cast shadows in shifting gradations of light, as if captives of the old cylindrical space into which he's refused to go. He's sure he won't see the others for a long time, seems not ever again, since only their shadows remain, cutting, shading and altering light in the frame of the trapdoor. He slumps back against the wet, porous rock of the cement wall, feels the sharp angle of iron in a doorframe jab his spine, and then slips inside it, farther back, knees wobbling, until he finds himself inside an electrical substation, curiously outfitted with a small wire-woven cot and a musty gray Red Army blanket. He quickly buries his face in the old Soviet fibers and ashen scent of time.

His father stands in the threshold of the open door to their apartment and gives him a stony look behind his black horn-rimmed glasses. He half smiles, lips part slightly. He goes inside and holds the door open. When he tries to get past his father, he grabs him and kneels next to him.

What happened to your shoes, boy?

I don't know.

The soles of your shoes are melted! Where were you playing?

THE WORLD IS ENDING YESTERDAY

In the woods.

Boy, I told you to stay out of those woods.

His father rises and looks at him, looks him all over. He looks so long he remembers looking at himself: his grass-spotted knees, dark sooty hands and arms. His mother comes out of the kitchen and he can sense her terror as his father marches him into the dining room, tells him to lie on his stomach on the carpet. He grabs the hand-sewn fringe of the carpet, feels the cool rubber backing in his hands. He hears his father's belt whipping out the loops of his dress slacks, the buckle ringing lightly in the air. His father jerks his pants off.

You ever going to do that again? his father says.

No, he replies.

Then, Wop! And the stinging . . .

You ever going to do that again?

No!

Wop.

You ever . . . ?

Wop.

No! No!

I don't believe you.

Wop.

I won't! I won't!

Ever again . . . ?

Wop.

No! No! No!

The whipping goes on a long time, until he rolls onto his back and tries to wriggle away, at which point the tongue of the belt buckle strikes him between his eyes. It hurts so much he coughs instead of screams. Then it doesn't hurt. His father stops, everything stops, and his father stands over him.

Jesus, his father says, I've told you before. When I'm whipping you, don't turn around. Now look what you've done to yourself.

His father's head blacks the light fixture above so it looks like the dark center of a full eclipse. Then the blood runs from his forehead into his eyes. He is amazed that red blood in his eyes seems so black. He is also astonished that every time he shouted No!, that he wouldn't ever do it again, his father didn't believe him and hit him all the harder. All he can think is that he is receiving two punishments. One for the thing he's done. Another for things he might do, even when he's said he won't do them. Then he reasons: if there are two punishments for every crime, he must have two fathers. One father who punishes, for he certainly punishes him. And a second father who fears, for he certainly fears he will do it again. And the only time his two fathers come together is after the whipping in the full eclipse of his father's head by the ceiling light.

Lying there after the whipping, his mouth is open and he's terrified he might have a slight smile on his face, that his father will see it. But he doesn't say anything. His father doesn't help him up from the floor. He doesn't want him to. His father leaves and goes into the bedroom. He pulls up his pants, rises, and goes into the kitchen for a glass of water. His mother follows him, all the while pressing a damp washcloth into the wound between his eyes. While he drinks his water, she takes down his pants and kneels behind him. She starts to cry, yanks his trousers up, and goes off to get a bandage. Once alone, he gets a new idea. If he has two fathers who punish him, one for what he's done and one for what he might do, then he reasons he may as well be two sons, one who never does anything for fear of being punished for what he does, and one who does whatever he pleases for fear of being punished only for what he might do. It's two fathers—and it's two sons.

Oscar has hold of his shoulder. "Up you go, old boy." He shakes him vigorously. "Rise and shine." He gets one eye open and sees Oscar looking around himself at the darkness and dank of the substation. "Well," Oscar adds, "at least rise."

When he opens his other eye, he spots another sign on the opposite wall, Russian with English spray-painted beneath.

REMINDER! BRIGHT LIGHT WILL BE OUTSIDE!
PREPARE YOUR EYES!

They negotiate the tunnels of the old ICBM installation back to the surface. The guide warns them to shut their eyes after they reenter the light, then open them gradually. While they wait just inside the exit, Oscar's pacing again, though this time not picking and prying at the Mississippi fractures in the cement.

When they board the microbus back to the Hotel Crater, he feels sleepy, hollow, and now realizes that in such drowsy states he has a bad habit of following where he's led, and so he resignedly trails Oscar to a seat next to him.

"So your old man was a rocket scientist," Oscar says gruffly, his voice seeming to swoop in and dive-bomb his ears.

He ventures his gaze out the low porch of his palm, shielding his eyes from the garish sun glancing off Oscar's white shirt and his eyes that glimmer with an obscene moist cheer. Not sad eyes like Lincoln's. But like Teddy R's. Rough Rider eyes. Oscar fiddles with his mechanical pencil. His eyes jaunt back to the scar on his forehead.

"Rocket scientist," he mumbles, trying to forestall another of Oscar's questions.

The microbus makes an unexpected right into a small grove of trees, follows a tire-grooved dirt road, then plunges in and out of a deep rut. When it lurches right, over the pink-gray surface of a half-buried boulder, he knocks his head on the window.

Oscar quickly turns to him and taps a spot on his own forehead with two fingers. "Ouch," he says.

"It was my head hit that window," he explains to Oscar, "not yours."

Back at the Crater, he follows Oscar's "Beer's on me," this time to the bar in the basement. Oscar brings the beer in tall flared glasses, seats himself, and buries his upper jaw and nose into the frothy head of his glass. "Well, Yank," he gasps, pausing for air, "these beers are better than sleeping the day away at the Crater, right?" He slurps a little more foam. "Wow. That was really something. A real Soviet I-C-B-M site. You suppose we'd ever get to see an old site like that back in the States?"

Oscar waits for him to respond.

He waits for Oscar to go on.

Oscar starts staring once more at the indentation between his eyes, his little capital 'G.'

"I read about those Titan boosters in the 1960s, how U.S. nuclear deterrence depended on the enemy's knowing you can deliver the warhead on a Titan II from a distance of over 5,000 miles. This article said it's like 'bragging that you can throw a golf ball into the mouth of a teacup 150 yards away, and hoping no one ever asks you to do it.' Do you think that's about right?"

Oscar waits again for him to reply. Sets his beer in front of him. Looks around the bar. Then goes on.

"Anyway, imagine if that rocket intended for Cleveland," Oscar says, "well, you know, had actually found its mark!" Oscar pauses, leans a little across the table, closer, to get a better look at his forehead. Oscar starts laughing all by himself, then stops laughing the way people stop when they realize they're laughing alone. He lowers his gaze from the impression in his forehead to the top of the table. "There'd be nothing left today." Oscar shakes his head incredulously. "That's something."

He stares back at Oscar. He's waited a long time for the right moment.

He raises his glass to his lips, pulls hard on his beer, and sets it back. "All right, you want to know." Before Oscar can resist, he seizes Oscar's hand and presses the tip of Oscar's index finger to the depression in his forehead. When he feels Oscar relax the muscles in his hand, he tightens his grip on Oscar's finger and applies its tip with even more force. He feels Oscar's finger bone between his eyes, cold, stiff, and certain. "I'll tell you what it is," he whispers, leaning in close. Oscar's lips tighten. The cheery light in his eyes flickers out. "Mark of the rocket scientist." He releases Oscar's finger bone and watches the young man's hand slip to his lap, out of sight. "That's for waking me up," he adds with venom and gets up to go. "And don't call me Yank!"

Morning, and in his splendid half-sleep he is *not* on the bus south to Šalčininkai, the "Cold Land," where Oscar claims another SALT missile site's open; and another, south of that, in Dieveniškes, "God's Country." He is *not* vaguely aware of Oscar at his side saying something about how it's nice to have him "along for the ride," adding, "Yank—oh, sorry." Oscar's Rushmore shadow is *not* darkening the flickering blood-red pools he sees under his eyelids brought up by the bright light pouring in the bus window.

In his lingering half-state, the day yet contains infinite possibilities.

The world ends today.

The world will end tomorrow.

The world has ended.

Only a few moments left before the world's most annoying young man rouses him from reverie for good. He has to be quick. Forget about connecting the dots. Any part of the world, the story's the same:

The world is ending yesterday.

The truth is in his mother's cupboard.

A handful of Ohio Blue Tip Matches, strike-anywhere.

Robbie Sparks and he in the forest south of their apartment complex, hornets' nests, honeysuckle, wild cherry trees, some limbs off-shooting low on trunks, easy to climb. One match to his sneaker and he lights up dried grass and watches each blade combust, curl, and touch the next, until rings of flame crawl outward from a single blackening center. The fire spreads quickly. He and Robbie run the circumference of the fire-ring, stomp the flames, and tear apart burning limbs of bushes. Soon, they climb a cherry tree in the middle of the ring. Robbie lies on the branch next to him, his head blocking the sun and encircled by a golden crown of flame. They find a city of caterpillar tents among the branches, dew-dropped, sparkling. Robbie tears a branch from the tree, strips its leaves and begins bashing the tents.

"Come on, NASA Kid," Robbie says.

"Don't call me that," he replies.

He watches Robbie thrust the branch into the city of caterpillars, twirling it until caterpillar silk sticks like white cotton candy and grows into great fibrous wads. Caterpillars rain from their tents onto the brush fire below, sizzling, squirming, dying.

The world is ending—what to do?

He looks down into the burned-out hull of black grass surrounded by scorched bushes, then all around at the tatters of caterpillar tents flapping in the breeze. Hornets buzzsaw in all directions, making improbable, zigzagging turns. He leaves Robbie below, climbs higher into the tree, moving branch to branch, quivering the way frightened animals quiver knowing they may never make it down. He wonders if he wipes out all the caterpillars whether he may himself replace his two fathers with a single feared and fearless father. No more twos of this and that. No more twos of anything. No more confusion. The forest will be wild, lonely, brightly lit by reflected rays of the setting sun, trees casting long blue shadows, all in rank. There, in the highest limbs of the wild cherry tree he will pause before the remaining caterpillars asleep in their tents, their tiny, black somnambulant bodies, two parallel yellow stripes the length of each, bright blue dots alongside each stripe. There, before his deadly hand, they will curl in all configurations imaginable, entangled in their shrouds of sleep, like some foggy alphabet of life ready to form new words. Words never before spoken. Words that might have saved the world. Words before the whip, the buckle, and the crater.

WENDELL MAYO is author of four short story collections, recently *The Cucumber King of Kėdainiai*, winner of the Subito Press Award for Innovative Fiction. His other collections are *Centaur of the North*; *B. Horror and Other Stories*; and a novel-in-stories, *In Lithuanian Wood*. He's recipient of the Premio Aztlán, an NEA fellowship, and a Fulbright to Lithuania. Over one-hundred of his short stories have appeared widely in magazines and anthologies, including *Yale Review*, *Harvard Review*, *New Letters*, *Missouri Review*, *Prism International*, and others. He teaches in the MFA and BFA programs at Bowling Green State University.

CPSIA information can be obtained
at www.ICGtesting.com
Printed in the USA
FFOW04n1317040318
45351467-46019FF